Adventure House
Presents

SPICY MYSTERY STORIES

May 1942

This reprint edition is a facsmile edition. Variations in print
and quality are mostly attributable to the rough woodpulp
original this reprint edition is based on.

ISBN: 1-59798-029-3

This limited pulp reprint edition
© 2005 Adventure House

Published by Adventure House
914 Laredo Road
Silver Spring, Md 20901
www.adventurehouse.com
sales@adventurehouse.com

SPICY · MYSTERY · STORIES

May, 1942   Vol. 12, No. 2

CONTENTS

SPICY MYSTERY STORIES is published by the Culture
Publications, Inc., 900 Market St., Wilmington, Del. The
publisher assumes no responsibility for return of unsolicited
manuscripts.

In the Interest of National Defense Spicy Mystery Is Now Printed on Thinner Paper—
But Will Continue to Be One of the Largest All-Fiction Magazines Published.
AS BIG AS EVER—ONE HUNDRED AND TWENTY-EIGHT PAGES IN EVERY ISSUE!

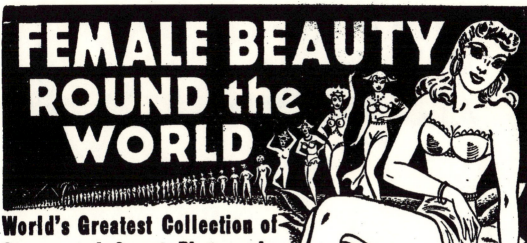

FEMALE BEAUTY ROUND the WORLD

World's Greatest Collection of Strange and Secret Photographs

NOW you can travel round the world with the most daring adventurers. You can see with your own eyes, the weirdest peoples on earth. You witness the strangest customs of the red, white, brown, black and yellow races. You attend their startling rites, their mysterious practices. They are all assembled for you in these five great volumes of THE SECRET MUSEUM OF MANKIND.

600 LARGE PAGES

Here is the World's Greatest Collection of Strange and Secret Photographs. Here are Exotic Photos from Europe, Primitive Photos from Africa, Torture Photos from Asia, Female Photos from Oceania and America, and hundreds of others. There are almost 600 LARGE PAGES of Strange & Secret Photographs, each page 57 square inches in size!

1,000 REVEALING PHOTOS

You see actual courtship practiced in every quarter of the world. You see magic and mystery in queer lands where the foot of a white man has rarely trod. You see Oriental modes of marriage and female slavery in China, Japan, India, etc. Through the intimacy of the camera you witness the exotic habits of every continent and the strangest customs of life and love in America, Europe, etc. You are bewildered by these large pages of ONE THOUSAND PHOTOGRAPHS including 130 full-page photos, and thrilled by the hundreds of short stories that describe them.

5 GREAT VOLUMES

The SECRET MUSEUM OF MANKIND consists of five picture-packed volumes (solidly bound together for convenient reading). Dip into any one of these volumes, and as you turn its pages, you find it difficult to tear yourself away. Here, in story and unusual photo, is the WORLD'S GREATEST COLLECTION OF STRANGE AND SECRET PHOTOGRAPHS, containing everything from Female Beauty Round the World to the most Mysterious Cults and Customs. These hundreds and hundreds of large pages will give you days and nights of thrilling instruction.

Contents of 5-Volume Set
Volume 1—The Secret Album of Africa
Volume 2—The Secret Album of Europe
Volume 3—The Secret Album of Asia
Volume 4—The Secret Album of America
Volume 5—The Secret Album of Oceania

Specimen Photos
Various Secret Societies—Civilized Love vs. Savage—Exotic Rites and Cults—Strange Crimes, Criminals—Omens, Totems & Taboos—Mysterious Customs—Dress & Undress Round the World.
1,000 Strange and Secret Photos

FORMERLY $10
NOW ONLY
$1.98

FOR THE COMPLETE 5 VOLUME SET — ALL FIVE VOLUMES BOUND TOGETHER

SEND NO MONEY

Simply sign & mail the coupon. Remember, each of the 5 volumes is 9¼ inches high, and opened over a foot wide! Remember also that this 5-Volume Set formerly sold for $10. And it is bound in expensive "life-time" cloth. Don't put this off. Fill out the coupon, drop it in the next mail and receive this huge work at once.

When answering advertisements please mention SPICY MYSTERY STORIES

In that silence he was sure that no one could have come up unheard, but there she was— lovely in the moonlight.

Maiden of Moonlight

By WILLIAM B. RAINEY

WHERE the road crossed the river and began to climb into the hills, Charlie Adams drove his car off the highway and hit it behind a clump of sassafras and blackjack bushes. For a while he stood looking at the rough, forbidding country ahead of him. He had come just in time, he thought, for there was only two dollars and twenty-five cents left in his pockets. "Well, there's gold in these here hills," he said aloud, smiling. "At least there is for me," and he started walking.

It was about twilight, the path gloomy beneath overhanging trees. A full moon hung white in the deepening blue of the sky and now and then bits of moonlight sifted down through the trees. The path climbed steeply until, suddenly, it leveled out in a small clearing.

That was when he saw the girl —or thought he saw her. She was standing at the edge of moonlight and shadow. At first glance he thought, *My God! A girl without any clothes on!* And then he thought it was just a trick of moonlight and shadow, and nobody

She was the most lovely thing he had ever seen—a woman to drive men mad! Anything she wanted he would do for her— and all she wanted was for him to kill, and kill, and kill. . . .

there at all. And then, for another instant, he was sure it was a girl: Tall, slender, with skin the golden color of a rising moon, and hair as black as moon-cast shadows, long hair that fell thick about her shoulders and formed a gauzy covering for the lush, high breasts.

Then the girl, or the illusion, was gone. It had been a trick of his eyes, he thought. Or perhaps there was a creek there in the trees and the girl had been swimming naked. But he didn't remember any creek close by. . . .

HE WENT on across the clearing and now he could see the cabin, crouched against another steep rise of hill—a one room, unpainted, pine board cabin. The windows gaped open, without screen or glass. One corner of the roof sagged and there was no light from inside. It didn't look like the place that a man worth nearly half a million dollars would choose for home.

But then his uncle Hank Hardee had never been like other men, Charlie thought. Charlie and his mother had lived here for a while when Charlie was just a child. Even then he had wondered why a man who had dug a fortune in gold from the earth should live in this filthy backwoods shack, hoarding his money, keeping it buried around the clearing, never spending it.

Well, some of it was going to be spent soon, Charlie vowed. He needed money and all at once he had remembered the uncle about whom his mother had never spoken except with a frightened whisper. The old man was nuts, of

course; a crazy miser. But there would be ways of making him come across.

No dogs barked as Charlie approached. Uncle Hank had never kept a dog because he would have had to feed it. Charlie knocked on the sagging door and called, "Hello, Uncle Hank!"

There was no answer. He knocked again.

And now he heard something inside the cabin. A movement, a whisper, he couldn't tell. He pushed the door open and looked inside.

Moonlight from the door and windows, and a dull bed of fire on the hearth made murk of the darkness inside. Through this he could see something creeping slowly toward him. And all at once he was afraid.

It was not the kind of sharp, physical fear that a man can fight against. He did not even bother to put his hand on the gun in his pocket; somehow he knew instinctively that the gun was of no use against this thing. If he had kissed a woman in the dark, thinking her beautiful, and then a light had come on and he had seen that her mouth was eaten half away with leprosy, he might have felt as he did watching this thing creep toward him.

Then the old man loomed up in the moonlit doorway.

He had been a big man, but now he was shriveled and gaunt. His clothes hung in rotting tatters. His shoulders humped forward and his head wobbled in front of them like the head of an old, sick animal. His dangling arms were little more than bones covered by shriveling skin. There was a froth of saliva at the corners of his mouth and in his eyes there was complete madness.

"Go away!" he said hoarsely. "Go away quick!"

"Uncle Hank? Hank Hardee?"

"Go away. You go away or I'll kill you!"

The fear in Charlie had turned to a sick revulsion now, but he forced a smile. "You don't remember me, Uncle Hank? I'm your nephew, Charlie. Your sister Martha's boy."

THE old man swayed. Terror came into his eyes and his mouth worked so that saliva drooled down across his chin. "I thought y'all was back east somewhere. What you want here?"

"Mama's been dead for ten years. I came out to stay with you for awhile."

"You can't stay here!" He screamed the words.

"Momma and I stayed here for a little while when I was just a brat. I remember a little about it. I've always wanted to come back."

The fear in the old man's eyes was a living flame now. "You wanted to come back here? Why'd you want to do that? What you want here?"

"I just want to visit you for awhile."

"You can't!"

"Well, at least I'll have to stay overnight," Charlie said, and to stop argument he pushed past the other and into the cabin. The old man followed, making whining pleading noises like the noise a dog makes when it wants to be let indoors. Charlie paid no heed. He put more wood on the fire and, as it blazed up, he looked around him.

There was no furniture. A few battered pans and buckets hung on the walls. In one corner of the dirt floor was a pile of filthy quilts. It looked like the bed of an animal rather than the bed of a human being. On the hearth before the fire was a scattering of gnawed bones.

"I'd like some supper," Charlie said. "It's quiet a walk up from the highway, and I haven't had anything since noon."

"I ain't got nothing."

"How about pancakes? Anything."

"I told you I didn't have nothing."

Charlie stared at the old man. God knew, he looked starved. But even a miser would spend enough on food to keep alive.

"I had a rabbit yesterday," the old man whimpered. "But I've et all of it."

"Why don't you go into town and buy some food?"

"I can't."

Charlie's laughter had a harsh sound. "You're worth a half million dollars—and you can't buy food. Don't lie to me. I remember what momma said, and I've checked. You've got money enough buried around here to buy all the flour in Texas."

The old man hunched farther forward. In the light of the fire his face was like that of a dog, Charlie thought. A mad dog. "So that's what you come for!"

"I might as well tell the truth," Charlie said. "That's what I came for. I'm your only relative and you've got more than you can spend before you die. I want some of it now."

"It wouldn't do you no good," the old man whined. "You couldn't spend it."

Charlie laughed. "Maybe you can't, but I won't have any trouble."

"But you can't! It—it ain't . . ."

"Just give it to me and watch."

"I won't do it! It's mine! I won't give it to nobody!"

Charlie's jaw set. "I'm going to stay here until I get some of that money. Five thousand dollars. That's all I want now, and you'd never miss it."

"No!"

"Then I'm staying until I find out where it is and take it for myself."

THE old man began to whine again. He walked back and forth across the cabin. Twice he went to the door as though about to leave but he hesitated, afraid of what he might see outside. Then finally he turned to Charlie again and his eyes were crafty. "Wait 'till morning. I'll give it to you."

"Now you're talking sense. I've got to have the money, but I didn't want to cause trouble."

"You just go to sleep. I'll give it to you in the morning." He lay down on the pile of dirty quilts, not pulling them over him but simply curling up the way a dog does. And like a dog he appeared instantly to go to sleep.

Charlie sat down on the floor before the fire and watched the old man. Curiously, there was no elation in him at the thought of the money he was to get. Rather, he had a feeling there was going to

She cried, "Keep away from me! You— I'm scared of you!"

be trouble. The old man had consented too easily.

Charlie said softly, "Haven't you ever spent any of the money, Uncle Hank? Not for food, or anything?"

The old man did not answer. He lay with his eyes closed, apparently asleep.

Charlie said, "You must have some neighbors now. I thought I saw a girl on the other side of the clearing."

The old man sat bolt upright, his eyes wild. "You—what?"

"Saw a girl. She didn't look as if she had on any clothes. Fact is, she looked something like an Indian, though I didn't know there were any Indians hereabouts any more."

"What—what did she say to you?"

"Nothing. She just disappeared. I couldn't be sure I saw her."

The crafty, deadly look came back in the old man's eyes. "You must of been drinking. Ain't nobody in thirty miles of here. Now just go to sleep and I'll get you that money in the morning."

The fire burned down until it was only a dull spot of color against the darkness. The moonlight was blue silver through the windows. The night was still, too still, Charlie thought. It was like a dead thing. No owls cried from the woods, no crickets, no frogs. The cabin, the clearing around it might have been swept back into some long dead age where the only living things were the two men and the only sound that of their breathing.

The silence pressed like lead against Charlie's eyelids. He

didn't want to go to sleep. He was afraid to go to sleep. And yet he could feel himself sinking into sleep like a man drowning in a bed of black feathers.

THEN he was awake. The room was pitch dark except for one small patch of moonlight. In the darkness something had moved and awakened him, but now it was still. He could not even hear the old man's breathing now.

And then it came like a storm. A deep intake of breath, a cry and the thing was on him. Fire lashed along his upflung arm. Something snarled and bit at him, screamed at his throat. The odor of ancient, unwashed flesh was in his nostrils and he writhed on the floor, fighting against the thing. A new lash of pain slashed his left hand.

He rolled into the patch of moonlight and could see. His uncle was on hands and knees a foot from him, a long butcher knife in his hand. With a snarl the old man dived at him, lashing out with the knife.

Charlie had not time to think. His left hand clutched at the old man's wrist and with his right fist he struck, hard. The blow caught the old man in the chest, and he collapsed. He lay on the floor moaning while Charlie picked up the knife, got the fire to burning brightly again, and made sure that his cuts were not deep.

He looked down at his uncle, lying still as a whipped animal upon the dirt floor but looking up at Charlie with eyes of unspeakable hatred. "So you were going to kill me," Charlie said, "to keep from giving me five thousand dollars. All right, now I want ten thousand."

The old man kept glaring at him, but he said, "I'll get it for you now, if you'll go away."

"I'll go away," Charlie said.

"I'll get it. You stay here."

He went out and Charlie let him go fifty feet before he slipped out and followed. He wasn't going to take any more chances.

The moon was so low that only a rim of it showed above the trees beyond the clearing. Where it touched the earth it was like quicksilver spread thinly on a table of darkness. Charlie had to follow the old man as much by sound as by sight, but he was close enough to locate the noise when his uncle started digging. He stopped in the shadow of some brush and waited.

The striking of the shovel was clear, distinct. It might have been the only sound in all the world except the dull thud of his heart, the whisper of his breathing. There was no breeze, no rustle of a leaf stirring or any of the myriad night sounds he was accustomed to.

"So you have forced the old man to dig up some of the money for you," the voice said.

He was so startled that he almost screamed as he whirled. And then he stopped, his heart high in his chest, his eyes wide with disbelief.

He would have sworn that in this silence no one could approach without being heard, but the girl was standing there close behind him, at the edge of moonlight and shadow—the same girl he had seen as he first entered the clearing. She was not completely nude, he realized now. She wore a narrow girdle of soft, beaded leather. Her hair, black as a crow's wing, fell loose over her shoulders and through it he could dimly see the curve of her breasts, ripe and firm. Her legs were long and tapering, full and lush in the thighs, small kneed. She wore beaded moccasins and in her black hair there was a single white feather.

He got the lump out of his throat. "I— You are the same girl I saw when I first came tonight."

"I didn't know then who you were. I didn't know you were going to stay."

"I'm not. At least, I hadn't figured on it before I saw you."

"I think you will stay."

She was staring at him with a passionate, hungry look. And yet, deep in her eyes, there was such hatred that seeing it he retreated a step as though she were about to attack him. She said again, "I think you will stay. They always do."

"Who does?"

She smiled curiously. "The old man is the only one here now."

He said, "You are an Indian, aren't you? I didn't know there were any Indians here anymore."

"The last of them died years ago, killed or made into slaves by the white men."

HE LOOKED at her, feeling a weird storm of emotions inside himself. Her skin was a golden bronze, even in the moonlight. Her face with its high cheekbones and full, primitive mouth was the most beautiful, most sensual he had ever seen. Through the curtain of her dark hair her breasts stirred with her breathing and, watching her Charlie could feel something growing in him like a flame.

She took a step toward him. He could see her breasts more clearly now. Her lips were parted and moist and her eyes intent on his. "You must kill the old man!" she whispered.

He could only stare at her. "What?"

"You must kill him. Then all the money will be yours!" She moved so close that her breasts almost touched him. Her eyes were terrible with their mingling of passion and hatred. "After you have killed him, I will be yours," she whispered.

The blood was beating thick in his throat. He reached for the girl, but she stepped back. "Will you kill him? Will you?"

"Why do you want him killed?"

Her laughter was intense, pulsing, but somehow insane. "Perhaps because I like for white men to kill. Will you kill him for me?"

"You're crazy," he said harshly. "I'm getting money from him, and I can get more when I want it. I don't want to be hanged for murder. Why should I kill him?"

"No one would ever know he was dead. No one would care. And he is old. He's suffered all he can. But he's clever. He's killed them all, because he knew they would come back and he had his traps ready. So you must kill him now."

She stepped close to him. "Will you kill him?" She put her hands on his body. "Will you kill him for me, so you will have all the money —and me?"

He was trembling. Her breasts touched against him. Her arms

slid around him. Her face was turned up to his, savage and passionate. Then he was tight against her, crushing her to him, swaying, half-crazy, muttering as his mouth pushed against hers, "Yes! Yes, I'll kill him!"

She broke away from him. "Hurry! There is so little time! The moon will be gone. . . ."

"First . . ." He tried to catch her again.

"Not until you've killed him."

HE WENT reeling away from her. His whole body was filled and aching with desire for the girl and he could think of nothing else. He was like a man blind drunk and obsessed with only one thought: To kill and return to her.

Then he stumbled on the place where his uncle had been digging. But the old man was not there.

He stared around him, wondering which way to search. And as he moved first in one direction, then the other, the terrible urgency of his intentions began to leave him. He began to feel sick and cold.

In the west the moon had gone down. The east was gray with dawn. Looking about, he found that the girl had disappeared.

"I was going to get myself in one hell of a lot of trouble," he muttered. "And for some Indian slut. . . ." But his mouth felt dry and the fear was still in him. He wanted to get his money and get away from here.

His uncle was at the cabin when he returned. Wordless, the old man held out a batch of old fashioned, big paper bills and Charlie counted them. "They are old, but they're still good," Charlie said. "I'll be going now. But to show you I appreciate this—there's an Indian girl around here who hates your guts for some reason."

The old man did not answer. "All right," Charlie said. "It's your business."

There were streaks of sunlight in the sky as Charlie crossed the clearing and started down the long, rough slope. What had happened during the night seemed like a dream, although he knew it was no dream because he could not forget it. One moment he was thinking of the Indian girl, of her slim, golden-colored body, and feeling desire begin to fill him again; the next moment that reasonless fear would be in him and he would remember the insane hatred in her eyes, and all he would want was to get the hell away from here.

There was a half bottle of liquor in the pocket of his car, and once out on the highway he uncorked it, took a long straight pull, then another, and a few minutes later still a third. In his empty belly the liquor seemed to wash back and forth with little waves of fire. The morning sun was hot and strong and the road began to waver a little. *I better get some sleep,* he thought, and pulled over to the side of the road.

IT WAS late afternoon when he awoke. He had been dreaming of a golden body throbbing and eager against his, of the girl's savage, p a s s i o n a t e, and hateful mouth. *I'm going back and see that wench,* he thought, and his hands were trembling as he started the motor.

She slapped him and he grabbed her arm, but then the man from the kitchen was coming with a knife.

But he hadn't eaten in more than twenty-four hours and hunger was gnawing at his stomach, so he drove toward the city. No need to get in trouble chasing after some crazy Indian girl, he told himself, when he had ten thousand dollars in his pockets. With that much money he could have plenty women of any color he chose.

But first he wanted food.

The restaurant was famous for its food and its prices, but prices don't bother a man who has ten thousand dollars in cash. Charlie was scarcely through the door, though, before the headwaiter was at his side saying politely, "I'm sorry, sir, but the place is full. We can't serve you."

A glance showed Charlie a dozen empty tables. The headwaiter was urging him toward the door but Charlie shrugged loose. "Why the devil can't you serve me? I'm hungry."

The headwaiter's tone was as polite as ever. "Scram, bum, or I'll call a cop."

"Bum? Damn it—" Then he saw himself in a wall mirror and stopped. He was unshaven, his eyes redrimmed, his face dirty from travel. He had forgotten how he must look. "Okay," he said, and walked out.

The next place he went was a hashjoint and he took a white-topped table near the wall. The waitress wore a green uniform in which her breasts made full curves, and as she went away, after taking his order, the dress wobbled lusciously over her hips.

"That's the dish I need," Charlie said to himself.

His mouth watered as she started serving him. His stomach twitched with emptiness, but he restrained himself from attacking the food before it was all before him. To keep his eyes off it he looked at the waitress. "What time do you get off tonight, baby?"

She didn't answer but turned away to take some dishes from the next table. As she did a man passed, going out, and pinched her in passing. She turned and looked at Charlie with her lips tight across her teeth. "Dammit!" she said, "I've had all I'm going to take from you bums in one day!" and struck him full in the face.

"Hey! I didn't—" She started to strike him again and he was erect, clasping her arm so that for a few moments they struggled back and forth.

"Joe!" she called. "Joe!"

The man came from the kitchen, fast. He was a big man with a knife in his hand and he rushed straight at Charlie. Charlie backed away. "Look out!" he cried. "I wasn't the one pinched her! I wasn't—"

"Get out, you—!"

"But I—"

The man kept coming with the knife. "Get out!"

CHARLIE went. He was angry now, and he was a little afraid too, though he didn't yet remember the reason for his fear. There was still one big drink in the bottle in his car, and he gulped it down. For a moment he thought he was going to be sick, and then he thought it didn't matter whether he got food or not, what he needed was liquor. The hunger was dulled, but it was still there, and, passing a cafeteria, he turned in.

He went down the line, filling his tray with everything they had to offer. He took pie and cake, roast, steak, and liver with onions, potatoes and beans. He knew he couldn't eat it all, but he could eat what he wanted and money didn't matter. His tray was stacked by the time he reached the cashier.

A door back of the cashier opened and two policemen came through. One said to the cashier, "That's all, bud. The Department of Health is closing you up."

The other cop grabbed Charlie's tray. "Wait!" Charlie cried. "I—"

"If you'd seen this guy's kitchen you wouldn't want the food," the cop said. "Go somewhere else."

Charlie tried to argue, but it was useless, and he turned miserably out of the building. He went lurching along the dark street and through his mind, over and over, ran the words of his uncle:

The money wouldn't do you no good. You couldn't spend it.

That was crazy, he told himself. It was crazy to keep remembering it. His failures to buy food were just accidents that might have happened to anybody. But all the same it wasn't food that he wanted now. It was liquor.

THE bar had sawdust on the floor and a brass foot rail. There were booths along the other wall and from one of them came the high pitched notes of a woman l a u g h i n g drunkenly. Another woman, standing alone at the end of the bar, looked up with interest as Charlie entered, then looked back into her glass again.

"I want a drink," Charlie said. "A double one." He began to tug the huge roll of bills from his pocket. The woman saw it and her eyes got wide in her painted face.

The bartender slid the drink down the bar. As Charlie reached for it, the glass slid too far, tilted and spilled.

Charlie stared at the spilled liquor. He began to tremble a little. He said, "Another drink. And hand it to me."

The bartender looked at him. "What's wrong with you?"

"I just need a drink."

"Not here," the bartender said. "We been having trouble enough with the cops for selling to drunks. Come back when you're soberer."

"I'm not drunk. I—"

The woman had Charlie by the arm. "To hell with that guy!" she said. "Come on. Let's go some other place where we can get a decent drink."

Charlie went with her. On the sidewalk she said, "I got a room right down the block. And I got a whole bottle of liquor. Let's go there."

"Sure," Charlie said. He needed a drink. He needed something to stop this crazy fear inside him. Ten thousand dollars and he couldn't buy food, couldn't buy whiskey. . . . Just freak accidents. But he kept thinking of what his uncle had said—and of the girl he'd seen there.

He looked down at the woman beside him. She had blonde hair and her cheeks were heavy with rouge, her mouth crimson. He could see the white curve of her breasts in the deep V of the dress. This was what he needed, a woman's companionship and liquor, and he'd quit wondering if the reason his uncle had lived all these years in that mountain shack was because he couldn't spend his money, couldn't even buy food with it.

(Continued on page 90)

By
E. HOFFMANN PRICE

PRAYER to SATAN

D AN MASON, sitting on the scarlet Kurdish rug spread in Khosru Khan's reception room, looked out of the gloomy fortress and across the Sinjar Hills. From this distance, he could not pick out where he had pitched Howarth's camp, and he was glad that he could not. Finally he asked Khosru Khan, "What have my people done to offend you? For three days we have not had permission to take pictures."

Khosru Khan's deep set eyes and bleak face brightened as he regarded the angular American whose friendship with the Yezidi devil-worshipers was the occasion for Howarth's permission to bring his anthropological expedition into forbidden country. The *khan* answered, "So far, there has been no offense, but in the future, there will be."

Mason was not surprised. He

A prayer to the Master of Evil and Giver of Good!— whose shrine contained the silver peacock! An American received the prayer— and almost regretted his friendship for the Yezidi devil-worshipers

She said, "Whether you live or die, you will always remember me! Let us go into the pit."

said nothing, and struck light to a fresh cigarette. After a moment, the Yezidi prince went on, "Some of us can see into the future. Those people—" He gestured toward the far off camp. "Measure our height, and our weight, and the slant of our brows, and the distance around our heads. But they are not our friends."

The *khan* was right. Wilson Howarth, who had financed the expedition into the Yezidis' territory, believed that cash paid for everything; and so did his stooge, sandy-haired Brett. But Mason's job was to assure the security of the expedition, as well as to process the films. So he said, "They do not understand, they do not know you as I do."

Khosru Khan's eyes gleamed. "O Man! Neither are they your friends. Leave them, and become one of us."

"They are under my protection, just as I am under yours."

He knew these weird, fierce people; he knew that if he abandoned Howarth's expedition, loot and massacre would follow. Mason, Howarth's employee, was in command in the sense that a ship's captain, rather than the owner, is in charge. He was responsible for the safety of his employers, and then there was Diane, Mason's wife, who had insisted on coming with the party, instead of staying in Baghdad.

Khosru Khan smiled. "I say again, in that camp is not one person who is your friend. Go in peace, and may your eyes be opened."

MASON went to the arched entrance, where a leathery old Arab waited with two horses. A blind beggar squatted near the well and cried, "Alms, my lord, alms!"

Science could have prevented all this blindness. Mason, handing him a coin, could see better ways of spending money than to measure the cephalic index of a thou-sand odd Yezidis. He turned to the horse which Saoud was holding, when the beggar said, "O Man! Your blindness is greater than mine! For your gift of silver, I give you the gift of sight."

In spite of the blazing afternoon heat, Mason for a moment had the sensation of intense cold. It may have been that strange speech, coming right after Khosru Khan's words; but whatever the reason, he could not shake off the eerie conviction in the beggar's words. Mason said, "Give me your gift, uncle."

The man spat on the wet clay near the mouth of the well, and dipped up a daub of earth as though it were an ointment; then he came toward Mason with the wavering certainty of the blind, and said, "Close your eyes, that you may see!" Mason obeyed, and the voice went on, "Malik Tawus —Lord Peacock—Master of Evil and Giver of Good—you who have a thousand eyes, give this man the sight of two eyes!"

A prayer to Satan, the all seeing lord of the Sinjar Hills, whose shrine contained the silver image of a peacock! Mason started when a greasy moistness was daubed on each eye lid. The beggar chuckled. "It is too late! It is too late! O Man, now you have eyes that see, and you will see whether you wish or not! And go in Peace."

Saoud muttered, "I betake me to Allah for refuge!" His hand shook so much that the curb chain rattled when he held the Turko-man horse for Mason to mount.

A WEEK later, after the anthropological work had been resumed by Khosru Khan's permission, Mason had almost forgotten the beggar's gift. Once more, he was back at his routine, each night going into the stifling blackness of the double-walled tent where he processed the day's films. Saoud was helping him; and except for the faint and murky green light in the far corner, they worked in absolute darkness.

Trickling sweat stung Mason's eyes. He moved automatically, for he had spent weary days keeping Howarth and Brett from prying into the sacred shrine of the devil worshipers.

From the sweltering darkness where Saoud worked there came a choked groan, a rattling sign, then a thud. The old Arab had collapsed. Mason groped in the gloom, shouldered his muttering assistant, and carried him through the light trap into the glow of a rising moon. Then he started toward the headquarters tent to get a first aid kit.

There was no light. That was odd, for Brett usually worked at night, tabulating the results of the day's work. From within came the fumes of brandy; a man was snoring.

"Drunk as a hoot owl," Mason grumbled. "Swell expedition."

Then he saw the lights in his own tent, and saw the shadows on the wall. One was Diane's: long, shapely legs, and firm, high bosom. The other was a man, and before Mason's eyes, the two silhouettes merged, mouth to mouth.

"Are you sure he's drunk?" Diane asked, anxiously.

Howarth answered, "I ought to know, though you needn't worry, Brett's all right."

They sat on the edge of the cot now. Diane went on, "He might suspect."

"Who, Dan?"

Diane's laugh was soft and contemptuous. "He's too busy to know or care. I meant Brett—it'd be bad if he told Dan. He mustn't find out before we get back to Mosul."

And now Mason remembered the beggar outside Khosru's castle; through his wrath there ran a cool, bitter thought: *He did make me see!*

He saw more than the shadow of his wife and her lover; he saw why Diane had insisted on coming into the forbidding Sinjar Hills, why she had brought frail negligee and lacy nightgowns. She had been counting on his several hours in the field dark room, whose double walls blocked sound as well as light.

MASON took three quick steps and got a glimpse past the entrance of his tent. All he saw now was Diane's satin mules, and her lovely legs, and the trailing skirt of her sea-green robe. Then the lights blinked out; but in spite of the whirring of the wind-driven battery charger, he could hear her murmur, "Everything will be different when we—*oh, darling*—"

Mason halted, and his clenched fists opened. Since he had the gift of sight, he might as well carry on, and see all that was to be seen. Now that his moment of fury was spent, he sighed and relaxed; somehow, it was a relief to know what he had not permitted himself to suspect. Let them tell him in Baghdad. . .

He went to the headquarters tent and got Brett's bottle of brandy; that would give Saoud the needed lift. When he reached the processing tent, the old Arab was sitting up. *"Sahib*, devils choked me! It was not the heat, it was the blackness that they love." He rose, and stood steadily enough. "Now I go to help you, it is well with me."

Mason took a drink himself. He told himself that a prayer to Satan and a daub of clay on the eyelids had had nothing to do with his unexpected need to leave the darkroom; that Saoud, suspicious yet unwilling to be the bearer of evil news, had faked collapse, so that his master could see, and without being humiliated by sharing the knowledge with a servant.

When he left the processing tent, his own was dark. There were now lights at headquarters, and the usual bridge game was on. Diane looked up, fluffed her pale blonde hair, and let the sea-green robe slip well back from shoulder and bosom. Her arms were graceful, and she knew it.

"How did they turn out?" she asked, as usual.

Broad-shouldered Howarth and sandy-haired Brett echoed the question.

"Well enough. But—" He held out some damp enlargements. "Whoever made these shots of the Peacock Shrine ought to have his ears beaten off!"

Howarth's rugged face darkened wrathfully. "You're forgetting yourself, Mason. I took them myself. No one was around, and

it was a good chance. Folk dances and brats and sheepherders isn't enough; we need something sensational."

Mason spat. "You're likely to get it if Khorsu's tribe finds out! I warned you that I wouldn't impose on my friendship with him."

Diane cut in, petulantly: "Oh, do shut up! They didn't see him."

Mason was about to answer when, inexplicably, his glance focused on a heap of papers on the top of a filing case. He had not the least idea why his attention had been attracted, why he was no longer interested in explaining to Diane that her logic was far from fool proof. And he ignored Howarth, who said, with sudden amiability, "Better join us and have a drink, Mason; it's pretty stuffy in that darkroom."

From the corner of his eye, Mason caught the exchange of glances. His angle of vision seemed wider than before, abnormally wide. He stepped toward the low cabinet and dug into the heap. He found an ancient book which must have been thrust under the papers at the sound of his approach. The sudden tension which followed his move confirmed his suspicion; he had almost caught them with forbidden loot in their hands.

The covers were leather; the pages, vellum inscribed in unfading inks, a Kufic script illuminated in red and gold. He glanced at a column framed in exquisite scroll work, then demanded, "Do you realize that this is *Kitab-ul-Aswad*, the Black Book of the Yezidis?"

Diane laughed mockingly. "You have the sharpest eyes, haven't you?"

Through his wrath ran a cool bitter thought: "He did make me see!"

Howarth's jaw set. "Certainly. I'd hoped it was. And there are a good many other knicknacks in the shrine. The place is so sacred that the Yezidis visit it only a couple times a year, they won't miss it for months."

"You — damn' fool!" Mason growled. "I mean all of you."

Howarth jumped up. "Put that back. Who do you think you are?"

"As long as we are in the field, I am in command."

BUT Howarth was used to commanding, and the answer was all the more offensive for having been given in Diane's presence. He advanced, hand outstretched. "I'll take that. And if you're afraid, you can leave."

Mason set the book down. "Put 'em up!" he commanded.

"What?"

"I said, put 'em up." He smacked Howarth lightly. "Or suit yourself."

Then Howarth understood, and cursed furiously. Mason bored in with popping punches. He slashed and battered Howarth's face, half closed his eyes, cut his mouth: all this instead of knocking him cold. Finally, when Howarth stumbled and clawed the sand, Mason said, "Some people don't understand any other language. I'm responsible for a fool like you, and I can't duck the job till we get to Mosul. Diane, go to your tent, and start packing! Brett, have the men break camp, and get the trucks loaded."

"Where—where—what are you going to do?" Brett stuttered.

Mason picked up the Black Book of Satan's mysteries. "I am going to return this. Perhaps they have not missed it, in which case we have a very good chance of getting to Mosul without being massacred."

Howarth was on his feet, bleeding and shaky. "You mean—after all that risk—you're going to return it—you fool, there's not a single genuine copy of *Kitab ul Aswad* in the United States—if it's so dangerous — keeping it won't slow us down, since we have to leave."

Mason sighed, shook his head. "You still don't understand. I can't have my friends robbed. It's on my account that they allowed you here."

"They won't miss it," Brett protested, "but if you try to take it back, and someone catches you, then they will have it in for us."

"That is a risk you made—" His gesture included the two men. "I'll be careful as I can. Hurry, and you'll have a start, don't wait for me, I'll overtake you."

"You don't need to!" Diane flared. "Stay with your friends, you fool! If it were so deadly, he'd—they'd—never have been able to take it!"

There was no arguing with them, so Mason took the Black Book and went to have Saoud saddle two horses.

As they rode, a few minutes later, Mason passed his hands over his eyes, and shook his head. Try as he would, he could not convince himself that he had actually seen *Kitab ul Aswad* until after he had reached into a heap of papers. "That beggar gave me something," he repeated to himself. "And he told me it was too late to change the gift of sight. He meant that I'd see unpleasant things. . ."

THE shrine of Malik Tawus was some distance north of Khosru Khan's hilltop fortress; and Mason hoped, reasonably enough, to be able to replace the sacred book without detection. He scarcely expected Howarth to break camp and start at once for Mosul, and if he succeeded in his attempt, there would be no necessity. But even if not, he was determined to get the expedition out of the Sinjar Hills before Howarth and Brett risked another violation of the terms they had agreed to observe. He owed that much to Khosru Khan.

Presently, he recognized the barren peak, with its stumpy tower, and pressed on up a deeply shadowed ravine. Ahead was a patch of moonlight; and once more, Mason's vision became strangely acute. In spite of the brilliance reflected from the rocks, he perceived the lurkers in the blackness just beyond. There was a dull gleam of steel; sword or lance was to strike from the side, just as he reached the narrowest point of the cleft.

His first thought was that Khosru's men, warned of the approach of someone from Howarth's camp, had come to block the trail, so he called in the Yezidi dialect, *"Ana kurdim!"* and added, "I am under the *khan's* protection."

The answer was a blaze of pistol fire. The ravine exploded in a sheet of red. Mason barely felt the impact of bullets, nor the crash against the ragged rocks; his horse fell, killed by a wild shot. And though Mason retained scarcely more than a shred of consciousness, though he did not know whether he was dead or alive, he still was aware of things that happened there in the meeting point of shadow and moonlight, at the foot of Satan's hill.

There were triumphant yells, the sharp clatter of horses' hooves, and another shot. He tried to call to Saoud, but he could not; neither could he turn enough to see what was going on. He was not even sure that he was still one with his body, for he could feel nothing, neither his wounds, nor the sharpness of the rocks. But he could hear the mutter of the men coming from ambush rise to a quavering scream of terror.

His own wits reeled again. When he finally became aware of the moon beating into his face, he was shivering from desert cold; he was drenched with blood, and his body was one vast ache. Saoud was gone, and the horse which remained was dead. Then he saw the silvery shape, and marveled, and forgot his pain.

SHE was strangely dressed. A tall tiara rose from her hair, and a scarf bound her breast, though the fabric was little more than a silvery mist, like the close-fitting skirt which covered her from hip to a little below her knees. There was a soft tinkling of small bells, pomegranate-shaped, which fringed her skirt; there were gleaming pendants hanging from tiara to her smooth cheeks.

"I am Laylat," she said, in the dialect of the hills. "One of the hundred thousand daughters of Lilith, who danced before King Solomon, on whom be the Peace!"

Then Mason knew that the blind beggar's prayer had given him strange sight indeed: this girl who glided through the moonlight was one of the demons who prowl in the wastes. Saoud had often spoken of the *lilin,* who lure wanderers to madness and to doom in the desert.

Laylat knelt beside him; and now the moon was so bright that her frail garments hid none of her loveliness. Her wide, dark eyes were full of pity, and though he could not understand what she murmured as she touched his wounded head, the sound was soothing as the gentle contact. After what he had left behind him, he was grateful that a night-wandering demon and not any human being had come to see him die.

But Laylat took his hand, saying, "Get up and come with me, Dan Mason."

He tried to obey that soft-voiced, imperious command, and found that he could. It was unreasonable that he should be able to walk, but he went with her, without stumbling and without any pain. Soon he was entering the forbidden shrine, under the tower, where the Yezidis kept the sacred silver peacock.

The natural grottto had been roughly squared. The wavering flame of two unshaded lamps reached into the deep niche which housed Malik Tawus, the peacock god; and it was reasonable enough that Laylat, a demon of the night, should be at home in the shrine of Satan.

She said, "Dan Mason, you are on the border that divides life and death, and for a little while, you, like any man, can turn either way."

He was strangely unconcerned, perhaps because the offer was incredible, and because it was made in a smooth, sweet voice that made the present moment more important than the past or the future. Mason asked, calmly as though another person were concerned. "If this is every man's choice, why do so few take it?"

Laylat smiled, and he forgot that he had ever before seen a woman's smile. "Most of those who perish surrender to death because of weariness. They think they resist, but that is only blind instinct battling the inner soul's desire for rest."

There was no more pain or weakness in him, and he had ceased marveling at that. He looked for a moment into those wide, dark eyes, and touched her bare shoulders. She came toward him as his hands slipped slowly down her smooth back. "Can the dead walk with you across the hills?" he asked; and then, "Or do you only lead the living into the wastes? This is better than living, being with you."

"There is no promise that you can ever see me on any other night," Laylat answered. "That is the law of the *lilin*. Whatever your reasons for living, or not living, this night is ours."

He remembered the Black Book; it must be back there, with his dead horse. He had to make sure that Khosru Khan would understand.

"How does one live? There are still things I must do."

"You must pray to Malik Tawus, lord of the world. Since he is the master of evil, only he can turn aside an evil that has found its mark."

This was what the Yezidis believed: that Allah, contemplating his own perfection, has no thought for the world, and that Malik Tawus is his viceroy, near enough to hear the prayers of mankind. Mason turned toward the peacock shrine and asked, "What does one say?"

Laylat shook her head. "That is merely the image. You must go into the very Presence and demand life."

A prayer to Satan? The idea no longer seemed blasphemous, nor even shocking. Laylat took his hand, and led him into the dark-

"O daughter of murder! He cannot save your skin!"

ness beyond the feeble flicker of the silver lamps.

AT LAST she halted, tugged at his arm, and whispered, "Sit here, there is a bench. Before I lead you into the Presence—"

As her whisper trailed into si-lence, her supple body spoke to him in the blackness; her arms twined about him, and her lips found his mouth. He could no long-er believe that his body lay in the ravine beside a dead horse; that he was floating midway between life and death. He had merely stepped in some strange way from the laws of time and space, and he had in his arms not merely a woman, but the very essence of all women, Laylat, one of the daughters of Lilith.

And Lilith, they said in this weird land, had been the first wife of Adam. When at last their lips parted, and she nestled langourously in his arms, he knew why no human woman had ever erased the memory of Lilith from Adam's mind.

Finally Laylat sighed and said, "Whether you live or die, Dan Mason, you will always remember me. Now let us go into the pit."

The touch of her hand, the sway of her hip, the fleeting contact of her slender leg guided him down the stairs which spiraled into an incredible depth and darkness. Then, so gradually that he was scarcely aware of the change, an eerie half light melted the gloom, and Mason stood on the sandy floor of a vault whose crown he could not distinguish.

He glanced about. The curved walls enclosed only emptiness. There was no niche, no sculpture; only ancient rock, the heart of the hill.

Emptiness. A dead and meaningless shaft. He turned to Laylat. Her nails sank into his arm. "Wait," she whispered. *"He is here!"*

Then the bluish half-glow began to swirl in a vortex; it became a spindle, glowing and pulsing, stronger as it contracted. Energy radiated from it; fierce waves of power pounded and lashed Mason as though with physical impacts. All the eerie light which had been in the vault was now pulled into that one center, leaving unutterable blackness about him; and he had lost Laylat's hand. More than that, he had lost her presence, and he was alone. For the first time, Mason was afraid.

A voice spoke, though not to his ear. He felt the thought, and without the medium of words. "You who have come to ask for your life," the Presence demanded, "what will you do with it if you get it?"

The ferocious impact of the question stunned Mason; it blasted his mind as those bullets from ambush had shocked his body, though now all, instead of part of him, was paralyzed. The vault echoed with soundless laughter and monstrous mockery. "There is vengeance against false friends, and that yellow-haired woman," the Presence went on. "But what will you pay for the life that can be given? Do you give me their lives?"

The question was logical; but the implication terrified him. What could a man pay as the ransom for his unused span of life? His borrowed vitality left him. That fierce glow which seemed to feed on all the force about, taking and not giving, drained Mason's strength, and he could not speak; he could not stand. He clawed the floor as though to escape from that elemental fury.

Then Laylat spoke from the blackness: "Lord of the World, Viceroy of Allah, I speak for this man! In exchange for the lives of those who betrayed him, give him his life! He stands between life and death because he tried to spare when he should have struck."

For a moment, echoes mocked Mason. He tried to rise, to protest; but the Presense spoke: "You have given, and I accept!"

The vault shuddered from the great laughter that followed. Then the force and the radiance vanished. Laylat was kneeling beside him in the darkness, saying, "It is over, it is done, it is granted! And I do not have to leave until the sun rises. . ."

Dazed, he followed her up the winding stairs.

BACK in the shrine, Laylat set aside her tall silver miter, and unbound her long hair. She laughed softly as she caught his hand, and drew him to the dais beside her. "The old magic has not failed, the Lord of the World still listens to the daughters of Lilith."

She pressed close to him; she made his senses reel and dance from those more than human kisses. But Mason thrust her from him.

"They are fools," he croaked. "But they are under my protection, and I owe them their one chance."

He lurched toward the outer shrine; the wavering glow of oil lamps guided him, and then the moon outlined the arch of the grotto.

Soft, bitter laughter followed him as he stumbled over the threshold, and into the cold white glow that flooded the Sinjar Hills. "You live, but you can never forget the daughter of Lilith!" that sweet mocking voice called after him. "You live, and you have paid, for we were one when we faced the Presence. And now you lose me!"

Mason slid, rolled, leaped from one ledge to the next. Each step made him more aware of his wounds and of his weakness. But he reached the floor of the ravine, and found his dead horse.

The Black Book was gone; or else it lay in some dense shadow, and there were too many for him to search. He ran down the rocky cleft. After half a dozen strides, he came upon a scrawny Arab, lying face upward, staring at the moon. It was Saoud, throat sliced from ear to ear.

A ragged furrow seamed Mason's scalp. There was a wound high in his chest, and his exertions had made it bleed anew. But he had a chance of getting to camp, telling Howarth and the others of their peril.

As he saw it, he had been shot as a raider who had ventured too close to Satan's shrine. Khosru Khan's men must have recognized him, after firing that volley. And thus, seeing that they had shot Khosru's friend by mistake, they would have no scruple about finishing the party that was under his protection. Loot was loot, and now that the strangers had no longer had a friend of Khosru Khan as their protector, they were fair game. But there was still a chance that they had not yet raided the camp.

He stumbled on, breath coming in painful gasps. His head was splitting. As he wove and stumbled down the ravine, he was think-

(Continued on page 92)

Again and again, while Grayson sat paralyzed, the withered woman struck!

The CAVERNS of TIME

By JUSTIN CASE

The people of this region were not hospitable to strangers. But Grayson found one girl who was friendly to him—and a danger waiting for both of them

IT WAS a strange region, this into which John Grayson had thrust himself. Dark, deserted mountain roads had led him into it, through walls of silence as menacing as man-made barriers.

"What you want with the Jules, mister?" the woman asked.

Grayson fumbled the telegram from his pocket. It had been delivered yesterday at his hotel in Roanoke. "FELLOW NAMED CARLTON CLOUGH SUGGESTS YOU UPLOOK JULES FAMILY IN ENDONVILLE STOP IF ANY GOOD WE CAN USE AFTER ROANOKE BROADCAST GOOD LUCK TED."

A great deal, Grayson sensed, hung on his answer to the woman's question. These people were not hospitable to strangers. He said warily, "A man named Carlton Clough sent me. Do you know him?"

They exchanged glances. The old storekeeper shrank deeper into the shadows behind his counter. The woman rose. She was very old, very tiny. Her figure was that of an underfed adolescent, with a thin stem of neck, small breasts that stabbed the worn wool of her sweater. "You can ride with me," she said.

"But my car—"

"Can't use a car on the road we're goin'. It will be here when you come back for it." She held the door open, waiting, and Grayson felt himself drawn toward her hostile eyes.

Was it his imagination, or did he hear the silver-bearded old storekeeper whisper, "If you come back!" It might have been the wind.

Outside, he stood shivering. This little shack was like a candle-flame in a vast cavern. He was loath to leave it, especially with so dubious a guide. From the blackness of a nearby shed he heard the clump of a horse's hoofs, the squeal of sled-runners on hard-packed snow. A lantern winked. He saw the woman seated on what appeared to be an ancient buckboard fitted with steel slides.

"Get up, Mister Grayson!"

He climbed to the seat beside her. The litttle store vanished.

IT WAS hardly a road. On both sides the darkness was filled with the wind's whining. They climbed, and Grayson began to wonder if the ascent would ever end. The winding ruts reached their zenith; the horse pawed for his foooting. Down they went, and ever down, the woman's withered face set in a grin that gleamed in the lantern-light.

They stopped, to rest the animal. Grayson fumbled matches and a cigarette from his pocket, leaned forward to strike a light.

The woman caught his arm. He jerked his head up to find her staring not at him but over the horse's head into the crowding dark.

Suddenly she snatched up the lantern and blew it out. And Grayson heard the sounds which had caught her attention. Someone was approaching.

The woman's hand touched his wrist. "Be careful!" she warned. "Say nothing!"

Grayson thought he saw a shadow climbing. From her perch beside him the old woman bent backward, gathering something from the belly of the wagon. It was a whip, its black coils sleek as those of a snake. With it she dropped soundlessly into the snow and glided forward.

"Stand, Judie!" she shrilled.

The advancing figure halted, raised its head, and Grayson saw the white mist of a frightened face in which two black eyes widened as though to burst. A girl's face, young and lovely. Back she stumbled, her arms upflung for protection.

But the whip was swifter than her weary feet. It uncoiled about her thin cotton dress, lashed through the fabric and viciously caressed her back and shoulders. Again and again, while Grayson sat paralyzed with astonishment, the withered woman struck. She was an expert with her hellish weapon!

The stricken girl sank to her knees, moaning, her bare shoulders glowing dimly in the dark. The whip sought out her tender skin, exploding against it with savage pistol-cracks. Her white breasts tautened with agony as her hands sought feebly to cover them.

Finding his voice at last, Grayson shouted hoarsely, "Stop it! In God's name, stop!" And she stopped—but because she was finished, not because of his outcry.

She flung the whip into the wagon and lifted the whimpering girl in her arms. Without compassion she threw the girl, too, into the wagon, then clambered back to her perch and snarled a command to the horse.

Numb with amazement, Grayson looked over his shoulder at the pitiful shape. The moans and sobs had ceased. The girl lay in a huddled heap, her half-clad body cruelly exposed to the bitter cold. And she was beautiful. Not merely attractive, but beautiful! The perfection of her shoulders, the soft, pale loveliness of her young breasts, the matchless shape of her slim, bare legs . . . Grayson saw these things as in a fantastic dream, and felt them deep within him. The mere sight of her made his blood race.

He said darkly, "Damn it, your treatment of this girl calls for an explanation!"

The withered woman turned her head to stare at him. "You were not asked to come here, Grayson. Meddling, even in thought, is not tolerated by our people." Then she was silent.

AN HOUR passed. They had traveled far, climbing a mountain and descending deep into a black valley. Ahead, windows glowed in the rambling shadow of an ancient farmhouse, but whether the house stood alone or was one of a community, Grayson could not know.

The wagon stopped. A door opened and light spilled out. A man stood there, waiting. He spoke to the withered woman, then strode forward, black-bearded and grotesquely tall, to lift the whipped girl from the wagon. Grayson warily followed the withered woman inside.

A strange room, that! Oil lamps of a forgotten era burned on a massive table. A great stone fireplace yawned darkly. Room and occupants were mellow with time!

There was the withered woman, muttering in a strange tongue as she knelt before the fire. There was the tall, bearded man, grimly dropping his limp burden to the floor. And the girl, conscious now, her dark eyes aglow in a pale mist of face; her small hands clasped over soft, trembling breasts, her lovely shoulders red with the welts of the whip.

Who were these people? Not Kentuckians, surely! Why in damnation hadn't Ted Jeffery supplied him with more information concerning them? How was he to talk to them, make them understand him, without knowing their background?

Grayson wet his lips. "You—you have been very kind. I'm sure I can reach the Jules place without troubling you further, if—"

The man stared, scowling. The woman turned. Awkwardly, Grayson hurried on: "If you will just tell me where the Jules live—"

The woman said gravely, "This is where the Jules live. Here." Then she added, "I'm Sarah. This is my husband, Fletcher. What you want of us, Grayson?"

Grayson recovered slowly from his amazement, and was instantly on the defensive. Talk to these people of a weekly radio hour known as "This America"? Explain to them, or try to, that he, as advance man, wished to make friends with them so that Ted Jeffery might interview them on a nation-wide hookup? Ah, no!

"Why, I—there's nothing I want of you," he said desperately. "You see—ah—Carlton Clough asked me to come here. What he meant, I don't know. Nor will I until he gets here!"

The huge bearded man and his wife exchanged glances, and Grayson sensed with sinking heart that they were not pleased. Had he blundered?

"Very well," the woman said. "You are welcome to remain until he comes." She drew open a door to the left of the fireplace. "This will be your room, Grayson. Goodnight." She thrust a thick stump of candle into Grayson's hand, and shut the door behind him.

Grayson stared around him. The room was no larger than a cell. He tried the window; it was not locked. After a moment of indecision he shrugged, kicked his shoes off and threw himself on the bed. His eyes closed. He thought dreamily of the beautiful girl in the next room. He slept.

VOICES waked him, and he reared on his elbows, listening. But it was not English he heard, nor was it any of the half dozen tongues of which he possessed a trifling knowledge. There was an old-world formality in it, and presently he realized that a sizable group must be assembled in the adjoining room.

He crouched with an eye to the crack between door and frame, and what he saw amazed him.

Men and women of dark, swarthy complexion, occupied rough-hewn benches forming an unbroken circle. In the center stood the slender, white-faced girl whose beauty had thrilled him. Like a prisoner she stood, her dark eyes wide and wet, pale hands clasped to her ivory breasts.

One man sat apart, matted hair looped low on his brow, shading greenish eyes that never blinked in their cold scrutiny of the girl. The girl shrank from that gaze, as though it were an icy hand pawing the pale beauty of her body, twisting and squeezing her sensitive flesh.

Presently the formal discussion ended. As one, the group stared at the green-eyed man. He slowly stood up.

"You," he said, speaking in English to the girl, "are not one of us and never have been, though that can be changed. I shall forgive you for running away. I may later forgive your other faults. But before pity enters my heart, you must be punished." His thin lips flattened in what might have been a smile of anticipation.

The others nodded, murmuring their approval. The withered woman knelt, kissing the man's hands as though in gratitude. The girl shuddered, fighting back a sob of terror, and Grayson saw her tremble as though touched by something repulsive.

The withered woman said, "We thank you, Nicholas. We thank

His search ended as he came upon a girl
bowed before her torturers.

you for Judie's sake, too, though she has lost her tongue." Then Grayson heard his own name spoken, and saw them look toward his door. He retreated in haste.

A moment later Fletcher Jules entered and stood over him. "Rise, Grayson, and prepare to leave."

Feigning a reluctance to wake, Grayson rubbed his eyes. "Leave? But it's the middle of the night!"

"That cannot be helped. Dress yourself for the cold, and come."

The great room was empty except for Sarah Jules and her husband when Grayson emerged from his bedroom. They were waiting for him. The woman said tonelessly, "Whatever you may see or hear from this time on, Grayson, remember that our people will not tolerate interference from an outsider." With that she drew the door wide and motioned him out.

It was bitter cold. Ghosts of houses loomed and passed in the dark, but Grayson saw no lights anywhere. Perhaps the light of day shunned this place and left it *always* dark.

A larger building loomed apart from the others. Into it, through an empty meeting-room and down a dim flight of stairs, they went. At the base of the stairs extended a low-roofed tunnel. Along this in silent wonder Grayson walked for what he judged to be an eighth of a mile. Then he heard music and laughter, and was plunged suddenly into a scene of old-world gaiety that left him breathless!

MEN and women alike were dressed in glittering finery, dancing to wild gypsy music in a vast room that smelled richly of wine. The gaunt Nicholas was there, and others who had sat in judgment of Judie at the Jules house.

Grayson was swept into the abandon of merrymaking. Despite his reluctance he was whirled from one group to another as the music leaped to swifter tempo. He looked for Judie in vain. Around and around the room he danced, deafened by the din, winded by the exertion.

But now to his ears came a sound that stiffened him. Others heard it, too, and for an instant the heart of the festival seemed to cease beating—but only for an instant. Led by Nicholas, the dancers quickly resumed their abandon. But Grayson stood motionless.

Again it came, the sound of a girl screaming. What had Nicholas said? She must be punished . . . !

Grayson retreated stealthily around a huge platform at the rear of the room, toward a door there. No one challenged him. An instant later he was prowling along a narrow tunnel, his way lit by a lamp he had seized.

Guiding him now were the girl's screams, brilliant with agony.

On he went. A lamplit cavern broadened before him. He stopped short, staring. His search was ended.

Naked, or nearly so except for a thin girdle of black that clung loosely about her, the girl Judie knelt in an attitude of supplication in the center of the chamber, her wrists held high by ropes reaching from the ceiling. Her head drooped. Her dark mass of hair flowed like black water about her shoulders, curling down to veil, but not hide, the flawless ivory of her breasts, the soft, sweet lines of her body.

Flanking her, armed each with a whip, stood two grim females garbed in somber black robes. The whips rose and fell with mechanical, monotonous rhythm across the girl's arched back. At each vicious caress, she screamed in agony.

Breath hissed from Grayson's mouth as he leaped. Blind with rage, he scattered the women, seized a whip from one of them and drove them back. The whip cracked about them as they fled.

He turned then to the kneeling girl. In a moment her wrists were freed and she lay in his arms, so soft and warm and thrillingly lovely that he could not believe she was real. He gazed tenderly into her ashen face and clumsily wiped her tears. "They'll never whip you again!" he muttered. "Never!"

Her arms crept about his neck and he thought that she smiled. At the same time, knowing the danger of this place, he looked for a way of escape and saw an opening in the far wall. With the girl in his arms, he strode toward it.

She stirred a little in his embrace, her white body warm and soft as a kitten. "I—I can walk, Grayson," she whispered, "with some help from you. Together, perhaps we can escape. There *is* a way out from this place; that I know for sure!"

But Grayson did not hear. He was staring at the opening, at the grim shapes crowding it. He put the girl down and turned. Other silent shapes moved slowly from the tunnel by which he had entered. He was trapped.

It was a good fight, and a surprisingly long one. He did his best. His heart and soul were in it, and the nearness of the terrified girl—her courage as she fought beside him—gave him the strength of ten men. When at last he staggered to his knees under the onslaught, he was too weak to rise again.

One of the men, Fletcher Jules, stood over him and spoke angrily in the tongue Grayson did not understand. The others nodded, muttering their agreement. But the gaunt Nicholas, gazing at the girl, spoke in English.

"My people ask that you be dealt the final punishment, and the stranger with you," he said. "But we have another law that they forget. No man may knowingly lay his hands upon one of our women except he take her unto himself for always!" A smile crookedly touched his mouth, and the green eyes glittered. "It is my hope that you will enjoy being this man's bride, for his bride you shall be, if only for one brief heartbeat of time!"

SURROUNDED by the swarthy men of the valley, Grayson was marched back to the great meeting hall. Gaiety was dead there. Those who had not joined in the hunt for him were seated now in silence.

Grayson was marched to the platform, Judie with him. Nicholas stood before them. "Kneel!"

"I kneel to no man!" Grayson muttered. But heavy hands forced him down, held him there.

Judie knelt beside him. Then began a ceremony so strange that Grayson wondered if he were dreaming.

Nicholas began a chant, and the valley people joined with him. About their dolorous singing was something mystic, less of flesh than of soul. Grayson glanced at the girl, wondering if she too would join with them, and she did, but her eyes, unlike those of the others, were not tight shut, her hands not crossed upon her breast.

She leaned closer to him, and he felt her slim, warm body against his as her hand covertly sought his own. Though her lips scarce moved, a whispered message reached him.

"I am to be your bride, Grayson, through no choice of either of us. But know this: If choice were mine, I would kneel with you gladly. Remember that, when I am taken from you as is their custom. I shall not want to go, Grayson! My heart will die within me. Save me from it, if you can!"

Grayson squeezed her fingers. God, she was lovely! In this dim light her kneeling body was a thing of wonder, molded from dreams. His gaze caressed the proud beauty of her youthful breasts, the flow of her ivory thighs. He could feel the warmth of her like a drug. Give him half a chance, and he would have this girl for his bride in the manner of his own people, not hers!

The chanting ceased. Grayson stared at what appeared to be a giant pair of manacles in the hands of Nicholas. Advancing, the gaunt man looped a golden ring about Grayson's neck, then did the same to Judie, linking them like slaves. Words flowed like molten metal from his lips.

Now the valley people shed their silence. A mighty shout rose. Gay music set them to dancing!

With a look of wonder, Grayson turned to the girl beside him and rose, lifting her up. "By their quaint custom we're evidently man and wife," he said. "Well, their custom will do until another comes along!" He smiled into her eyes. "Is it also their custom for the lucky fellow to kiss his bride?" he mused.

His arms went about her, and the delicious, trembling warmth of her yielding body made him oblivious to all else. Here was beauty! Here was the lure of all womankind wrapt in one slim, quivering girl. His girl! His to caress, to possess. His bride!

Cupping her chin, he tilted her face to his and sought her parted lips. But at that instant, with a bellowed roar, the giant Nicholas thrust between them.

"Blasphemer!" thundered Nicholas. "Know you not it is forbidden to touch the bride! But no . . ." and his voice softened with mockery . . . "our ways are strange to you. You have much to learn. Drink, Grayson. Drink to your bride, to your future!"

From the rear of the platform came a young and lovely girl, near naked, holding a golden cup on a golden tray. Grayson took it and glanced questioningly at his bride. He saw her face averted, a tear on her chek. "Thanks, but I'm not thirsty," he said.

"Drink! Or it will be forced upon you!"

He was surrounded by swarthy shapes awaiting their leader's signal. Rage blazed within him. Then a hand trembled on his arm and his bride whispered brokenly, "Drink, or they will kill you."

"Is it poisoned?"

"No, Grayson."

"You ask me to drink it?"

Her lip quivered. The white, shimmering pearl of a tear fell from her cheek and ran slowly between her exquisite breasts. "Yes," she sighed.

Grayson drank, defiantly. The face of Nicholas blurred before him. Suspecting treachery, he sought within himself for pain but discovered only a pleasant languor. Faint were the festive shouts of the celebrants, dimmer still the tawny glow of the lanterns. From a distance he seemed to hear a woman sobbing—his woman, his bride, weeping in the

With a madman's strength he struck blow after blow.

tortured depths of her heart.

HOW much of what followed was reality, how much dream, Grayson could not know. He walked in a shadow-world of wonder. In and out of this alluring world weaved beautiful but disturbing phantasms.

Lovely young women, veiled only in pools of shimmering mist, paraded provocatively before him, their gestures an invitation for him to join them. Moonwhite of no form known on earth caressed their enticing bodies; stardust knitted diaphanous robes for their nude beauty. With them he walked through pleasure-paths of dream, their nearness arousing in him sensual hungers he had not known he possessed.

Time meant nothing in this mystic world. Yet there were momoments when some part of him rebelled at the delights of the moment. In these moments a face more beautiful than those of his tempting companions, a girlish figure even more alluring than theirs, struggled to intrude.

In time, he remembered her name. Judie, his bride! He heard voices, one the thin voice of the withered woman, Sarah Jules, the other her husband's.

"He dreams," the woman said. "They all dream, after drinking the wedding wine! Ah, what I would give to know of what he dreams!"

"Every woman would give her all to know the secret of the wine," Fletcher Jules mocked. "It is forbidden to ask."

"Aye, I know it. Nor do I ask. Nor would I answer, my love, if you were to ask of what I dreamed that night, while entertained by the Master; or of what other brides dream. More than most, I know what goes on in the Master's house, since to me is entrusted the privilege of keeping it in order."

Through the mists, Grayson heard them. They spoke not English, yet he understood. What powerful potion, what mighty lifter of barriers, had he consumed?

But now the woman spoke in English, mocking him. "Dream, fool! If you knew the truth, your joy would rot! We have strange customs here, Outsider. The one that now enslaves you is strangest of all. Shall I tell him of it, Fletcher?"

"He is asleep."

"Ah, but he should be told. Be happy with your dreams, Outsider, whatever they are. While you dream, your lovely bride belongs to another. When two are wed among our people, the bridegroom spends his wedding night dreaming—but the bride spends it in the arms of the Master! Do you hear, Outsider? Look, Fletcher. He scowls!"

"You imagine it."

The woman's voice faded, derisively taunting Grayson until silence took it. A door closed. Grayson's eyes opened. He recognized his surroundings and was mildly surprised. They had returned him to his bed in the home of the Jules.

Rising, he moved soundlessly to the door. Anger fought with prudence, and anger won. He flung the door wide. Sarah Jules and her husband whirled to face him.

"He is awake!" Sarah gasped. "But it is too soon!"

Grayson ploughed forward. His fist caught the big man flush on the jaw and felled him, and he caught the woman as she turned to flee. Holding her by the throat, he shook her.

"My wife. Where is she?"

More than rage widened her eyes as she squirmed. Fear was in them, and unless he were mistaken, a wondering respect for his courage. "Are you mad?" she whispered. "Nicholas would kill you!"

"I'll risk it! Lead on!"

She obeyed because she had to. Trembling in his grasp, she opened the door and stumbled into the night.

THE night was cold and black, but the woman knew her way. Soon, out of the darkness ahead, loomed the shape of a house larger than any Grayson had seen since entering the valley. Its great hand-wrought door was shut against intrusion.

"I can take you no further," Sarah Jules said. "The Master's door is locked."

"You have a key for it. You talk too much, woman!"

She plucked a key from her bosom. "I—I cannot take you to the Master himself, Grayson!" she muttered. "I know not where he is!"

"You came here on *your* wedding night, old one. Lead on!"

She crept forward. Grimly he followed through a series of well furnished rooms. "He—he is below," she sobbed, "in his chamber in the earth. May the Master have mercy on us both!"

They entered a small but rich room in which candles burned dimly, and now an uncomfortable sensation seized Grayson that he was being watched. He hesitated, while Sarah Jules stooped over a low table and her fingers groped for something Grayson could not see.

The creaking of a counterbalance startled him. Abruptly he stepped back from a section of the floor that swung swiftly open, revealing a dark chasm in which a descending flight of stairs was visible.

"Follow me," Sarah Jules whispered.

Down she went, into a darkness that lay in wait like some slumbering beast. With a sixth sense warning him, Grayson warily followed. One glimpse he had of the tunnel below, leading into abysmal gloom. Then a voice shrilled behind him.

"No, Grayson, no! That way leads to the pits!"

He flung himself back upon the steps as the voice was smothered. Judie's voice! But as he whirled, Sarah Jules caught at his legs.

Grayson's frantic kick smashed her full in the face, and she fell back, screaming. He leaped to the carpeted floor above, stumbled, caught himself.

"Well done, Outsider," said a voice slurred with mockery. "Dare you come the rest of the way?"

A chill touched Grayson's rigid body. The girl he loved lay in a sobbing heap across the threshold of a door which until now he had not known existed. Attired like one of the mystic creatures of his dream, in a diaphanous white web of gown that hid nothing, revealed all, she lay like an exhausted dancer, her white legs limp, white breasts faintly throbbing. She had warned him, and the Master had struck her down.

And now the gaze of the Master was on Grayson himself, dark and deadly with anger. The muscles of his huge body rippled under tunic and tight-fitting black trousers. His restless hands clutched a whip.

Grayson eyed the whip with misgiving. Fashioned of some flexible metal, it bristled with glittering

(Continued on page 94)

VERA-RAY
by WATT DELL

The agressor nations have established a base on the moon. Tom and Vera trap the crew of a huge cannon which is calibrated to shoot a tiny 22 rifle bullet at the earth. It is trained, with amazing accuracy, at the White House steps. Prof. Pryor, traitor to his country, forces Vera and Tom Parnell to assist him

I WILL AIM; PARNELL YOU LOAD AND VERA MUST FIRE

GO AHEAD, VERA... I'LL THINK OF SOMETHING!

I'D RATHER DIE; BUT WHEN HIS CREW REVIVES, HE'LL KILL ALL THE GOOD MEN ON EARTH.. PRYOR, YOU ARE A LIVING DEVIL!

CLOSE THE BREECH, PARNELL, AND COUNT THREE. THEN VERA, YOU PUSH THE PLUNGER.

Tom points to the helmets; Vera understands..

Tom leaves the breech open..- just a little.

ONE, TWO--

Vera pushes the plunger down. — a tremendous charge of powder drops into position behind the tiny bullet in the huge gun.

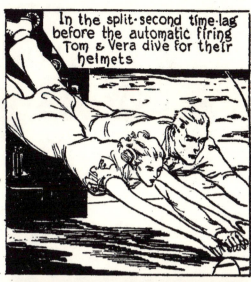

In the split-second time-lag before the automatic firing Tom & Vera dive for their helmets

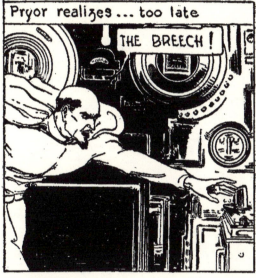

Pryor realizes... too late

THE BREECH!

The great gun back-fires and bursts like a bomb.

GOT TO WAKE UP... GOT TO GET VERA.. SAFE..

CAN'T BREATHE... HELMETS! SOON, AH! RIGHT HERE.. WE'RE SAFE!

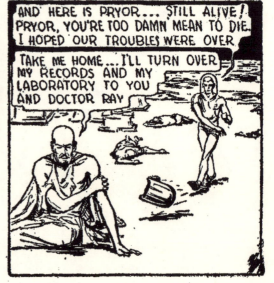

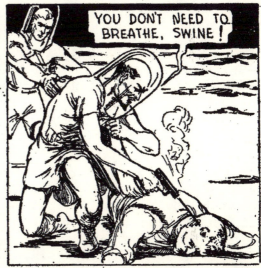

PRYOR HAS THE WHIP HAND. CAN VERA OUTWIT THIS MADMAN? WILL THEY BE ABLE TO LEAVE THE MOON AT ALL? _____ SEE THE NEXT ISSUE OF SPICY MYSTERY.

PAYMENT in BLOOD

By REX DALY

He could hardly believe the girl he loved was dead—killed in her own father's hellish experiments. But that was no harder to believe than other fiendish things that happened in the big house!

H E DETECTED the peculiar abattoir smell long before he caught his first glimpse of the somber house on the summit. The charnel odor puzzled him, made him uneasy.

Through gathering dusk the road wound its course up the timbered mountain; towering trees merged their shadows with a dank and ferny undergrowth, while down in the lowland a mist was eddying in from the surrounding sea. Dirk Greyling had an uncomfortable feeling that the fog was a living thing which would follow him to this high place and engulf him. He shivered, although he was not cold.

An hour ago his yacht had dropped anchor in the harbor of the little fishing village which was this Carolina-coast island's only settlement. His heart had been exultant as he hired the hamlet's sole conveyance, a battered and decrepit sedan, to bring him up here to Professor Linwold's isolated home. He'd been thinking of Lynne Linwold, the professor's gloriously beautiful blonde daughter, whom he loved. In anticipation he had tasted the sweetness of her parted lips and thrilled to the

yielding surrender of her welcoming embrace. It would be like regaining a lost paradise to hold her once again in his arms....

He was thinking of the old days, and of those well-remembered daily trysts with Lynne Linwold. He was remembering the firm pressure of her soft young body against his, the rippling tremor of her sleek length when she yielded to his caresses. And he was recalling the silly quarrel that had parted them; the quarrel which had sent him forlornly on a year's voyage in an effort to forget. Well,

She struck at his gun wrist, deflecting his aim.

it was no longer necessary to forget. Lynne still loved him—and she had sent for him! Why shouldn't his heart be exultant?

But now the swift onslaught of darkness and that persistent charnel-house odor sent a curious foreboding into his subconscious mind. And when the sedan's grizzled old driver halted his car with a clattering jerk, Greyling felt an intuitive inner warning that danger, nameless but very real, was not far distant.

"What's the matter?" he demanded. "Why stop here?"

THE oldster's voice held a hint of fear. "This is as far as I'll go, mister. I got no hankering to trespass on Linwold's mountain after nightfall. And if ye take my advice, ye'll let me drive ye back down to the village right now. Daylight's the time to come visitin' the professor if ye must come at all."

"You mean you're *afraid* of Linwold?" That seemed the height of absurdity to Dirk Greyling

He was remembering his college days, when Linwold had been one of his science professors: a tall, mild, doddery sort of fumbler with a passionate hobby for experimenting with the electrical generation of heat. Into one of his super-crucibles a stray cat had one day wandered, seeking warmth; later Linwold, not realizing the animal's presence, closed the crucible's door and stepped up the rheostat to full capacity. The cat, of course, had hideously died before a rescue could be effected; little more than a powdery grey ash remained when at last the crucible was cool enough to be opened. Greyling

was remembering how deeply moved the gentle professor had been by the gruesome mishap; it had seemed to prey on his mind for weeks, and he had spent many silent hours over the ashes of the cremated cat. . . .

A man so soft-hearted that he endlessly brooded over the chance death of an alley tabby was certainly not a person to engender fear in his neighbors, Greyling thought. Yet this elderly taxi driver seemed genuinely afraid. "I'm turnin' around and goin' back this instant, sure as my name's Jeb Farrand. *You* can do as ye see fit," he said flatly.

Greyling was irritated. "If it's more money you want—"

"All the money in hell wouldn't pull me closer to that gate," Farrand grunted. He pointed forward.

For the first time, Greyling noticed a high fence of galvanized steel mesh barring the road and plunging on either side into the concealing forest. He saw a metal gate in the fence, wide enough to permit the passage of a car; and all along the bottom strands of the mesh barrier itself there were small, motionless furry shapes—

The carcasses of animals, rotting and festering!

Then Greyling saw the red-daubed sign above the gate: "KEEP YOUR DISTANCE. HIGH VOLTAGE. DANGER!" And he suddenly realized the meaning of the stench which had assailed his nostrils as he approached. The fence was viciously charged, and hundreds of little woodland creatures had met swift destruction by accidental contact with the surging current!

It was so savagely unlike Professor Linwold to do a thing like that, Greyling thought. It was almost as fantastic as the newspaper stories which had appeared all over the globe a few months ago: stories to the effect that Linwold, now retired, had perfected an electric crucible capable of achieving such hitherto-impossible temperatures that commercial diamonds could be made from plain carbon. Later Linwold had denied this, and the rumor had died. . . .

"But how in God's name does a person get through to the house?" Greyling demanded out of the depths of his astonishment.

Farrand gestured to a box set upon a pole. "There's a phone in that thing. Ye call Linwold an' he cuts off the juice long enough for ye to get through—if he wants ye to come. The ones that don't get in are the lucky ones, if ye ask me."

"Lucky? Why?"

"Some has gone in an' not come back out, that's why! I've heard tell that Linwold bakes people in his ovens. Somethin' to do with makin' diamonds. . . . It may be just talk. I dunno and I ain't aimin' to find out." He peered at Greyling. "How-come you're so anxious to see the crazy coot tonight?"

"Why—I'm an old friend of his. Used to be one of his students. He invited me to visit him. I just received the letter a couple of days ago."

The letter hadn't been from Linwold himself. It had been written by his daughter; Greyling had found it awaiting him on his return from that twelve-month voyage. Postmarked and dated just a week before, it had seemed like a reprieve from lifelong loneliness and heartbreak. "I'm sorry we quarreled, Dirk darling," she had written. "Won't you forgive me and come to see us? Father joins me in extending the invitation. We've found the weirdest house on an island mountain-top, where he can conduct his electrothermal experiments. . . ." Then had followed directional instructions, which Greyling had followed without a moment's loss. . . .

Farrand clucked his tongue. "So the professor wrote an' invited ye? Hmph. Well, if I can't talk ye into waitin' until daylight, I'll be leavin' ye here. Ye may have a long wait."

"What do you mean?"

"Sometimes he lets ye ring the phone for an hour or more before he answers. Sometimes he don't answer at all. Seems like he's been actin' more cracked and queer than ever, these past six months. Ever since his dauhter, Miss Lynne got killed."

A STAB of uncomprehending bewilderment knifed through Greyling's heart; he couldn't believe his ears. They must have tricked him! "*What did you say?*" he shouted.

"I said ever since Miss Lynne got killed. The old man's daughter, ye know. Six months ago, 'twas. She fell into one of the professor's ovens an' he turned on the heat without knowin' she was in there. Leastways that's what he claimed. Hardly enough left of her to bury, as ye might say. Too bad. She was such a pretty girl."

"You—you're insane! Lynne

"Oh, God! Please!" she cried as the giant lifted her.

can't be dead! Why, I just received—"

Farrand shrugged. "Can't help what ye thought, mister. She's dead all right. I helped dig her grave. Well, so-long—an' good luck. Ye may be needin' it." He backed his antiquated car in a half circle and went clattering down the road. The sound of his clanking motor died faintly in the lower distance.

Greyling felt as if he'd been bludgeoned. Lynne . . . his beloved Lynne . . . dead! Dead six months or more! Dead as that cat had died in Linwold's college laboratory . . . roasted in a hellish crucible. . . !

But how could that be *when she had written a letter to Dirk Greyling only last week?*

Somewhere there was something fantastically out of focus. Professor Linwold's keen brain wasn't the sort that would topple into madness. In spite of the gossip, he couldn't be crazy enough to incinerate living people in an effort to create diamonds. Most certainly he wouldn't have deliberately murdered his own daughter, as Farrand had hinted. And yet . . . there was this charged fence that acted as a death-trap for the furry creatures of the forest. And there was Farrand's insistence that he had helped dig Lynne's grave. . . .

Perhaps there had been a mistake. Someone else had died in the crucible; not Lynne. Lynne was still alive, she had written a letter to Greyling just a few short days ago. *Or had she?*

He felt a sudden penetrating sensation of dangerous aloneness. The fog was drifting and thickening up the mountainside, as he had known

it must. And his surroundings were so somberly silent that the encroaching darkness was like a shroud falling. Beyond the gate, a sinister grey pile of stone masonry was Linwold's house, looming like a ghost against the dimming background. . . .

Lynne! Greyling whispered her name out of the depths of his dazed misery. Lynne . . . ! Never again to enfold her in his arms, savor the succulent moist sweetness of her lips, caress her lilting contours, feast his eyes on the glorious symmetry of her girlish body! Never more to delight in the piquant challenge of her starry blue eyes, the soft warmth of her breast throbbing madly against him in utter abandon. . . .

"It's a mistake! It's not true!" Greyling rasped. And he leaped toward the box which held the telephone.

He ground the crank with frantic energy; awaited an answer. None came. He twisted the thing again. But it must have been almost an hour before he heard a quavering, strained: "Hello?"

That was Linwold's voice, all right, but it had changed: There was no kindliness in it, no gentle warmth. Instead, there seemed to be a leaden lifelessness, a peculiar lack of inflection. Like the voice of a madman. . . !

"This is Dirk Greyling. I've got to see you!"

"Greyling . . . ? Oh, yes. Yes . . . I'll cut off the current. There. Now you may come through."

Greyling hung up; approached the gate. Just as he reached for its steel handle, a rabbit dashed past him like a hell-spawned thing. It struck the gate's interwoven mesh—

THERE was a flash of arcing blue fire, a sputter of electricity, a sharp tang of ozone intermingled with the stench of roasted flesh. The rabbit, burned almost to a crisp, dropped to the ground at Greyling's feet. He jumped backward. "God!" he whispered. In another instant he, too, would have been fried by that hellish current!

Linwold had lied when he said he was cutting it off. *He had tried deliberately to murder Dirk Greyling!*

Savage anger arose in Greyling's throat. Now, more than ever, he knew he must confront Linwold and demand news of Lynne. The old man was monstrously insane: a maniacal killer. He must be put away where he could do no more harm. . . .

Greyling unpacked one of his two Gladstones, yanked out a rubberized black raincoat. He found a long pole of deadwood and wrapped the vulcanized coat around it to insulate it. Then, cautiously, he poked the pole toward the gate; managed to unlatch the fastening. It swung inward.

Greyling raced through.

And now, with his heart hammering thunderously against his ribs, he pelted up the narrow roadway and at last gained the looming, sinister house. He bruised his knuckles on the massive front door.

It opened. A woman stared out at him. A brunette woman, lushly contoured in the full, seductive beauty of maturity. Her housefrock limned the sweeping lyre of her hips, stressed the full pouting prominence of her bosom. Her eyes were dark, unfathomable; her lips too red, too smiling. That smile was as false as a mask, Greyling thought. . . .

"My name's Greyling. I want to see Professor Linwold," he snapped.

"Why . . . why yes. Of course. I'm Miss Madden. Molly Madden —the professor's housekeeper. He's expecting you. I'll go get him." She conducted Greyling to a vast, gloomily-vaulted chamber smelling of must and dank decay; and when she left him there, he couldn't help noticing the feline sway of her hips and the muscular rippling of her thighs under the house-dress. There was an undeniable aura of lure about her—and a suggestion of grim capability—

He felt eyes staring at him, and he pivoted. He caught a brief glimpse of an apish black face, loose-lipped and evil, above a shambling gorilla-like torso. The hideous black man was passing the parlor's rear door and had paused to study Greyling with baleful intensity. Greyling took a forward step to confront this huge apparition; but the black scuttled away as silently as a wraith. Then, from the hallway door, Professor Linwold said: "Dirk, my boy! I—I'm glad to see you!"

HE WAS so changed that Greyling scarcely recognized him. His flesh had fallen away; he was little more than a living skeleton. In cavernous eye-sockets set deeply into his pasty, cadaverous face, his eyes held what seemed a feral glitter; his smile of greeting was a hideous counterfeit thing, unconvincing and peculiarly repellent.

Greyling ignored the older man's outstretched hand. "I want to know about Lynne," he said.

"Ah, yes . . . Lynne. Poor Lynne. She . . . died."

"In one of your crucibles?"

"Yes."

So it was true, what Jeb Farrand had said! A hopeless deadness slid through Greyling's soul; it was followed by a swift spate of rage. He wanted to shout: "You killed her, you damned maniac! You murdered her!". But he held the words in bitter check; he must not tip his hand until he had an opportunity to get away from this hellish house, return to the village and bring the authorities back to make an arrest.

Greyling knew that he could easily have handled Linwold; but there was that black man he had seen . . . a servant who might jump to his master's rescue. . . . That apish brute was twice Greyling's size; he might well be capable of carrying out whatever bidding the professor commanded. Such as throwing Greyling into one of the electric crucibles. . . .

So Greyling held his peace; stoppered the seething vials of his wrath. "Tell me about her," he said quietly.

"Come, I'll show you." Linwold led him down into the cavernous cellar of the house; it was fitted out as a laboratory, lined with huge electric ovens and thickly-insulated crucibles. Heavy power-cables crisscrossed the low ceiling, and curious pieces of apparatus hummed droningly in the corners. Greyling sensed that he was not alone with the professor during this trip of inspection; he felt that he was watched by sinister, hidden eyes. The black man's? That brunette woman who called herself Molly Madden? He didn't know . . .

Linwold gestured evenly toward one huge crucible set into the east wall of the cellar: an oven-like electric furnace large enough to have held a man. Its thick asbestos door was closed, and through heat-resistant glass set into the portal Greyling could see the interior glowing with hellish incandescent whiteness, blinding and evilly awe-inspiring. "Lynne died . . . in there," her father said unemotionally.

"Good God . . . ! But *how* did she get in there?"

"I don't know."

"And you've never torn the thing down? You go on using it?"

"I must go on with my experiments."

Greyling wanted to seize the man; wanted to yell: "So you don't know how it happened? I'll tell you. You threw her into that hell!" But again he choked back the words. . . .

God, he thought. This monster murdered Lynne—his own daughter—in that furnace! Killed her as that college cat was killed! Maybe the cat's death was no accident, years ago. . . . Maybe Linwold did it deliberately. . . . Maybe it was how he first hit on the maniac notion that diamonds could be produced from the carbon of roasted living flesh . . . !

Linwold said: "Of course you'll stay here with us tonight, my boy. You daren't risk going down the mountain in this fog. You might lose your way, stumble over a bluff. I'll have Miss Madden show you to a guest room. And . . . I'm sorry for you. I know how you felt about Lynne. "

The foul hypocrite, Greyling thought. Aloud he answered: "It was six months ago that Lynne . . . died?"

"Yes."

"Then how could she have written me a letter just last week?"

Linwold stiffened. "A—a letter? But that's impossible! The dead don't return to do things like that. Someone hoodwinked you with a forgery. "

"I know Lynne's handwriting!" Greyling answered levelly. But deep in his mind there was a horrid doubt. Had the letter been faked? Or—more fantastic still—*had it been penned by a ghostly hand? Was it a means through which Lynne's earthbound spirit had cried out for vengeance . . . ?*

O F ONE thing he was certain: Linwold was a madman. A murderous maniac. To place him

His fist struck her to the ground. "You would have killed me!" he snarled.

under restraint, Greyling must move cautiously; arouse no suspicions. "I'll be glad to stay overnight," he agreed.

Linwold cleared his throat nervously. "The letter you say you received: what did it say?" His eyes seemed oddly furtive, almost fearful.

"Not much. It invited me here . . . that's about all."

The old man allowed the subject to drop. And a little later, the brunette housekeeper conducted Greyling to an upstairs bedroom and left him there alone.

He didn't undress. In the darkness he threw himself across the bed, thinking . . . thinking . . . He must have unwittingly dozed, although he had planned on wakefulness; he felt that peril was very close, and he hadn't wanted to be taken by surprise. Yet sleep he did; and he awakened to the sound of his door slowly opening. He slid to his feet. He saw a shadowy white shape drifting toward him—

"Lynne! *Lynne, beloved!*" he cried hoarsely.

An infiltration of moonlight trickled through the window beyond his bed, and he could discern the ghostly pallor of her fair cheeks, the wan and corpse-like glaze of her lackluster eyes. She was clad only in a shimmering thin robe of some diaphanous material, almost the ectoplasm; her long yellow hair streamed about her shoulders, and he could see the hinted outlines of her swelling breasts, the flat slimness of her hips, the rounded, tapered perfection of her legs. . . .

"Lynne!" he said again. And he leaped toward her.

She backed off. "Don't touch me, Dirk. Please." Her voice was sepulchrally hollow.

He stared. Some weird moonglow trickery made her seem shimmering and evanescent, and for an instant he thought she might be a form conjured up by his own nightmare imagination. It was as close as he dared come to the thought that was really at the back of his mind . . . that she was of the spirit-world. . . .

And then he saw something that flooded his veins with relief. She *cast a shadow!* And ghosts don't cast shadows—

"You're alive! You didn't die six months ago!" he breathed. He reached for her.

"I am not alive. I . . . died. . . ."

The clammy deadness of her voice froze him.

She went on swiftly: "You must get away from here—before *he* kills you! There's just one chance, and you must take it now—while there's still time. A way through the charged fence . . . I'll tell you how to reach it. . . ."

"Not unless you go with me!" he said. And he caught her in his arms.

HE half-expected to close his embrace about nothingness; to have her fade and vanish before his eyes. It didn't happen. His seeking hands encountered warm, vibrant flesh. And when he pulled her against his yearning body, he felt the wild throbbing of her heart and the pulsating enticement of soft curves crushing on his chest. "God . . . you're *real!*" he sobbed in his throat. And he kissed her.

Her arms clasped about his neck;

she locked herself to him with a sudden spasmodic gesture, made no effort to stay the movement of his palms upon her shoulders and her back. He looked down and saw the wild surging tumult that stirred her rapturous bosom under the thin silk that covered but did not conceal. "Dirk . . . !" she whispered. . . .

The next few minutes were like an ageless bliss, whose memory could never die. Then, without stopping to ask the questions which churned within him, he drew her toward the door. "We'll go away — together. Explanations can come later."

"Wait . . . until I get some clothes. . . ." She vanished in the hallway's blackness.

MINUTES dragged. He heard a whispered: "I'm ready, Dirk." He tiptoed out of his room and felt a soft hand grasping his own. In that solid darkness she was an indistinct presence; almost a disembodied entity, he might have thought, had he not held her hand in his. She led him forward to a staircase; they descended. They went out into the moonlit night.

He froze. "You're not Lynne. You're the housekeeper—Molly Madden!"

The lush brunette nodded, hugged his arm close to her side. "Yes."

"But Lynne—she told me to wait for her—" He jerked free and started back toward the silent house.

The dark-eyed girl stayed him. "Wait. To go back in there means . . . d-death. For us both! Lynne didn't come to your room a while ago. *I did.* I wore a yellow wig. I—I knew it would be the only way I could persuade you to leave that hellish house! Now . . . you've got to take me away! I'm afraid! Afraid they might kill me . . . as they killed Lynne. . . ."

"You mean *you* came to me? It was *you* then, not Lynne whom I . . . ?"

"Yes." She hung her head as if ashamed. "It was the only way I could think of . . . Now come! We'll get through the fence. Then if you want to send the police back here tomorrow, we'll both be safe. . . "

They were at the electrified fence. She pointed to a spot apparently no different from all the rest of the barrier. "Right there. A secret latch. And no current at that point. Open it. . . ."

His arm snaked about her lissome waist. "One kiss more!" he demanded with savage fervor. She yielded it to him willingly enough, pressing herself so close to him that he felt the softness of her bosom flatten warmly against his chest. A moan escaped her—

He thrust her away, struck her across the cheek, viciously. "Damn you!" he snarled. "You weren't in my room. You think I don't know the difference between Lynne's kisses and yours?" He shoved her roughly toward the fence. "If there's a secret gate there and it's not charged—open it. *With your own hands.*"

She cringed. She fought like a tigress as he tried to push her against the fence. "No—my God, no—it'll kill me!"

"That's what you tried to do to

(Continued on page 98)

By
JOHN WAYNE

SEAGRAVE was buried alive, and he liked it. Mists rolled in over the low lying Mississippi Delta, obscuring the orange groves. The rusty screen kept the hordes of mosquitoes out of his cabin. New Orleans, though only sixty miles away, might have been on another planet.

When Seagrave slumped over the rickety table, and knocked his glass of absinthe to the dirt floor, the lovely Cajun girl brushed the jagged fragments into the hearth, then patiently coaxed him to sit up.

Louise had great dark eyes, and clear olive skin. A crimson rayon blouse shaped itself to her bosom, and cast a rosy reflection on the

Haiti Magic

*The mysteries of the living dead seemed only a dream
—a piece of superstition—until the girl he loved was
taken by those who walk by night.*

The girl who danced for the ceremony was
his dead wife!

curves that peeped from the yoke.
Louise Guérin's feet would never
fit into a 2-AAA last, but she was
all woman. And silk hose gave an
alluring finish to her legs.

"That is enough Pernod for to-day!" She mopped up the spilled greenish liquor that did not make Harry Seagrave ever quite forget the wife whose tomb he could just see, among the orange trees. "Now, here is the gumbo I 'ave bring."

Louise picked up the big bowl and set it on the table. Okra and rice, crab claws and ham and shrimp and oysters swam in the savory mess. Seagrave brushed back his black hair; gray fringed it a little more each day, ever since Marilyn had taken poison to avoid his wrath.

"I'm not hungry," he hiccuped. But the tang of *filé* and bay and thyme tempted him. He looked up at the shapely girl who leaned close to him. He dipped in the tin spoon. His sharp face brightened a little. "Say, that is damn nice, honey."

Louise was not a bit jealous of any dead wife. Like all the French natives of the Delta, she was too practical. And Seagrave owned thousands of acres; once a sugar plantation, but now gone to ruin. Her father had leased most of that flat, swampy ground along the Gulf. The bayous that threaded the outlying marshes were now planted with oysters, the best strain of oysters that the Gulf offered.

When he thrust aside the empty bowl, she followed him to the lounge that was near the open fire. Louise snuggled close, stroked his unkempt hair, and whispered, "You will not always have the grief, *chéri.*"

She was warm and plump, and the arm about his neck stirred Seagrave in spite of himself. Not even remorse and absinthe could resist Louise. Her dark eyes gleamed for a moment as she felt him tremble, hesitate; then her lashes fluttered, and she clung to him when he kissed her.

She had been waiting for that kiss for weeks. Patiently waiting. It was not good for a man to sit watching the tomb of a dead wife. And as men went, Seagrave was worth patience. He could read. He was a gentleman, before penitence drove him to the gay goddess in the bottle.

That first caress told Seagrave how much he had been missing. He ignored the eerie mists that swirled about the brick tomb, some yards beyond the plantation house that slowly crumbled to ruin. The red sun was drowned in the haze, but the lovers did not notice the day's end. . .

WHEN she patted her dark hair into shape, the world looked a little different to Seagrave. Maybe he had been a fool, going to pieces about Marilyn's suicide. He had not really driven her to it; but this was the first time self-justification began to convince him.

Louise smoothed out her skirt. It was thin, and clung to her legs, outlining their voluptuous curves. She turned to him smiling, and said something about being time to go home. It really was . . . in this nine o'clock, sleepy Cajun wilderness. . .

Louise's sudden change of expression startled Seagrave. Her smile froze. Then her eyes became round, and her mouth sagged. Her extended arms no longer invited him. They merely reached out.

She was staring at something beyond him. Seagrave shivered. He caught her contagious mood before she cried out, recoiled a pace.

"Look—over there—"

He whirled, took a backward pace. Louise clung to him. He had to support her weight. Whatever else she said was in Cajun French that he could scarcely understand; she was incoherent. And so was Seagrave.

In the swirling white mists and pallid moonlight, a whiter form was walking. It materialized from the tormented grayness between the orange trees, and came toward the negro cabin that Seagrave had reclaimed from ruin.

A woman was gliding from the grove. Her hair was silvered blonde. Her arms were crossed on her breast. She was slender, shapely; white throat, and white bosom peeped from the frail shroud that blended with the marsh mists which hid her feet.

"Marilyn—" The word came to Seagrave's lips, a choked, dry sound; his legs threatened to buckle. "Marilyn's—come back—"

He was all the more afraid when he heard himself say that. He had been drinking too long and too much. The pale green absinthe had made him see things even more outrageous than this, but thus far Louise had not seen them. She also must be crazy.

The white figure floated nearer. It seemed to ripple a little in the breeze. It was Marilyn. Her eyes stared. She was near enough to the window for him to see that. She made a gesture, with one hand; the other still was at her breast. The motion was as if a mechanical toy made the last move possible before its springs ran down. The eyes were dead and expressionless.

She brushed close to a small orange tree. The branch shivered. That evidence of solid flesh made the apparition even harder for Seagrave to face. A platinum band was on her finger. Nothing was missing as she stood there, pointing and wordless.

Then she turned, and slowly went away, hips swaying just a little, as they had during life.

"She's not a ghost," Louise said when she could speak. "She's a *zombi*. A living dead one."

Seagrave knew what that meant: a corpse resurrected to serve a necromancer, to work in the fields; a mindless thing whose unnatural animation made it more horrible than anything honestly dead. He had never heard of a white *zombi*, though in Haiti, black ones were common.

But this apparition which had invaded the gray fantasies of absinthe shocked him to the soberness he had not known for months. "Wait," he said to Louise. "I'm going out to her grave. I'll look!"

Louise whimpered with terror; Cajun superstition was shaking her. He would not stay, and she was even more afraid to follow him.

A S HE went into the swamp mists, he caught a peculiar, pungent smell; a sickening sweetish odor that reminded him he'd have to get some more mosquito repellent. They bit him unmercifully, as though they preferred him to the natives who had been hardened to the pests.

But Seagrave was remembering too many other things to think much of citronella oil and the like. He nerved himself to go toward the tomb in the orange grove. He was still too shocked to feel normal qualms.

Marilyn looked just as she had the day of burial. Gay, frivolous Marilyn, always dancing. Too many admirers; and Seagrave's jealous wrath. Whether justified or not, he never knew. About the time he loaded a gun and went out hunting Dr. José Castro, the most obnoxious of the crowd, Marilyn's protestations of innocence had ended in death during his absence. Her pathetic note had turned his wrath into remorse.

"... *maybe this will convince you ... it's wrong to take one's own life ... they won't bury a suicide in sanctified ground ... but you can put me into the family vault at the old plantation ... unless you prefer the cross roads...*"

Instead of giving her the complete obliteration that old traditions prescribed for the self-damned, he had followed her last wish. The thought that his injustice had driven her to death made him abandon his business, and move out to the plantation. Absinthe, and the brick tomb where the other Seagraves slept kept him company.

He did not know what had happened to the romantic Dr. Castro. The Cuban gallant had disappeared before Marilyn's burial. But his haste was wasted. Seagrave did not hunt him.

What most shocked Seagrave was that he could, here and there, distinguish the print of bare feet in the spongy ground; small feet, like Marilyn's. A tatter of shroud fluttered from the thorn of an orange limb. And then he saw the brick tomb.

Its door had been torn from the hinges. Bits of mortar lay white on the ground, and there were some dislodged bricks. He stood there making wordless sounds. The implication was too much for him. With supernatural strength, the resurrected dead had burst the vault open from the inside!

Seagrave turned and ran back to the house.

"The crypt's empty," he croaked. "She broke out!"

"It's my fault," Louise said, shuddering. "She's angry."

She slowly drew away, glanced over her shoulder. At the door, she halted and said, "She's angry. I'm afraid to go home. I'm afraid to stay."

Seagrave poured a tumbler full of brandy. The rental of the oyster bayous kept him supplied with plenty of liquor. Louise drained the glass. She smiled a little when he took some from the same bottle. It was better than that deadly Pernod which maddens people.

They faced each other, not knowing what to say next. Then Louise came to him, arms extended. "She's a *zombi*. That's not like a ghost. I won't let her keep me away."

It was a brave effort, but Louise's generous lips were cold as her hands when Seagrave took her in his arms. There was not a kiss left in either of them, and

From the grave she came toward him, uttering no sound. . . .

they stood shivering before the dying fire.

A curious scratching at the pane startled them. This time Seagrave was the first to turn. A black bulk blocked the window. Great black paws clawed at the sill, and white teeth gleamed. A monstrous Negro babbled and drooled outside.

Seagrave hurled a bottle. The pane smashed. He yelled, "Get out, or—"

He snatched the shotgun that he had never used for any hunting in the marshes. The blast swept away what remained of the window. Shot chewed away the sill and casement. There was a bestial howl, a squishing and thumping outside.

A black hulk shambled into the mists of the grove. Trembling, Seagrave ran to the sill with a candle. Outside, he could see the prints of gigantic splay feet. But there was no blood, no sign to show that the double charge of shot had taken any effect.

"You can't go home now," Seagrave said to Louise. "Not with

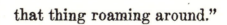

that thing roaming around."

THOUGH badly shaken by the uncanny succession of prowlers, Louise felt safer indoors than anywhere else. There was a question in her eyes as she regarded the narrow couch of the one room cabin. But her query was not to be answered at that time.

There were footsteps outside. Men were muttering. Dogs bayed. Someone cried, "M'sieu Seagrave! Don't shoot!"

The two inside exchanged glances. They both recognized the man's voice. Jules Boudreaux, the sheriff of the parish, was out with a posse. Seagrave gestured toward the big *armoire* in the corner; this was the only place where Louise could hide. While there might be some gossip about her frequent visits to the cabin, he did not want her made conspicuous at that hour.

As she ducked for cover, he went to the door. Lanterns made yellow blobs in the moon lighted mists that swept from across the marshes. Gun barrels glinted. Bearded men in boots and leather jackets followed the sheriff. Louise's father was close to the front.

"What's up, Jules?" Seagrave demanded.

They came in. Pierre Guérin, Louise's father, mechanically chewed his tobacco and forgot to wipe his chin. His leathery face was twitching, and his eyes flickered about the room. The others were muttering and shaky, but none as conspicuously so as Guérin.

The sheriff answered, "By God, it is terrible! The devil, he is making the rounds. He 'ave keel Simon Labadie's woman. Only the little girl is escape."

"What?" Seagrave was thinking of the monster who had clawed at the sill, only a few moments ago.

"We follow him with the dog. We hear the shot."

"I missed him," Seagrave answered. "He went that way."

Guérin's shifting glance spied the bowl which had contained gumbo. He recognized it. "Where is Louise?" he demanded. "When she leave?"

There was no answer from the closet. Seagrave played that silent hint. He answered, "Couple hours ago. Isn't she home?"

The oyster dredger's groan and gesture made Seagrave regret his well meant falsehood. The rugged fellow cursed him with a glance. Then he said, "If she ees kill—all torn up, like Labadie's woman— by God's, I keel you! What for you let her stay too late?"

Seagrave was an outsider. These hunters and oyster dredgers and makers of illicit orange wine ignored the law across the river. They ruled the parish, and their great grandfathers remembered Lafitte, the pirate. A tough crowd.

He ignored the direct query. He said, "Sheriff, whose nigger is it?"

Though there had been no slaves for three quarters of a century, every negro in that quarter still "belonged" to someone. Boudreaux answered, "It is no nigger. I tell you, my fran, is a *zombi*. You live too much by yourself. You have not heard. But the *bayous*—" He gestured to include the region. "The orange groves. Everything —the live dead, they are all over. By God, *monsieur* the devil is taking this parish."

"How do you know it's a *zombi?*" Seagrave did not dare mention Marilyn's uncanny resurrection, or they would clamp down on him as the cause of the curse that roamed up and down the delta. "What—"

"The drums. We hear them. There are lights in the bayou by night."

"You can't hunt down ghosts," he temporized.

Someone laughed nervously, and cut in, "It is not sure, yet, what this is. We shoot, but we do not hit him. You have the gun. Will you join?"

Seagrave could not refuse. Louise was his only excuse for staying, and when, later, he did take her home, she could account for her absence. She could blame it on the *zombis*. The superstitious Cajuns would accept that, readily enough. And she would be safe enough in the cabin, now that a posse was systematically combing abandoned sugar plantations and orange groves that furnished nothing but untax-paid wine. . .

The sheriff had come down from Buras, where cows blocked the highway. The other settlements along the dirt road that skirted the river were too small to find, except on a map. Fort Jackson, long abandoned by the army, was slowly being veiled by semi-tropical vegetation; corrosion claimed the guns, and all else made of iron.

For a while, the posse plodded across the level expanse of the old Seagrave plantation. Though a tangle of woods, the ground was level as a billiard table. Toward the further extremity, where levees still raised their bulk to keep out salt water when the Gulf was storm-lashed, were the abandoned cabins of the laborers who had once tilled the plantation. It was

here that the skulking *zombi* might hide out.

"What'll you do when you find him?" Seagrave demanded. He hoped that Louise would have enough presence of mind to bar the cabin. "If he's dead, he's dead."

They did not have a plan. Some were muttering and crossing themselves. Others pretended to discount the *zombi* idea entirely. Seagrave was certain that the entire posse was merely staging an act, each putting on a front to seem courageous in the eyes of his neighbor. One said, "If we cannot shoot and kill, then we give him something with salt. If he eats, then he runs to his grave and stays dead."

Cellophane crackled. The speaker had a package of salted peanuts. But Seagrave did not laugh. He had heard too many details of what had happened to Simon Labadie's woman. And he was still shaken by the sight of Marilyn.

THE cabins were deserted. But when the posse reluctantly moved on toward the little burying ground where the laborers had put their dead, there was a moment of silence. Something had made each weed covered mound erupt; some subterranean force had lifted and scattered the heavy earth. And the prints of splay feet were plain. A dozen *zombis* had left their graves! there was no mistaking the traces of big, bare feet such as no white man had.

The weather beaten faces of the posse turned gray in the lantern light. They eyed each other, and went into an apprehensive huddle.

Seagrave, standing on the levee, looked out over the level stretch of salt marsh that reached out to the Gulf.

The muddy bayous had a metallic gleam. Far out, yellowish lights bobbed and blinked; others were stationary. These marked the luggers and cabins of the oyster dredgers. Then he heard the muttering of the posse.

They were all more or less distant cousins. Those who worked along the river spoke for those who made their living in the bayous. If this continued, they would all leave, and let the Devil have the oysters!

The posse swung toward the river, making a wide arc. Seagrave could not break away. They would think he was afraid. Worse than that, they would suspect him, as a "foreigner," of having a hand in these uncanny events. So he accompanied them to Venice, the last hamlet on the road.

There he saw Simon Labadie's woman. They had laid her out, but little had been done to conceal the effects of the battering. Her throat was clawed. Nails and fangs lacerated her once comely face, and her glazed eyes still mirrored the horror that they had seen. Handfuls of her black hair had been torn out. Seagrave gulped and turned away when he saw that long nails had laid her scalp open. In a corner were broken chairs, and the walls were splashed with blood.

The print of a big, bare foot, clearly outlined by one of the stains, made Seagrave think of the erupted graves. The muttering Cajuns eyed him, and shook their heads. Thus far, they merely blamed his abandoned plantation.

The posse climbed into the truck in which Boudreaux and his deputies had come from Buras. Seagrave shook his head when they beckoned to him.

"I'm looking into this myself," he said. "If all the oyster dredgers leave the bayous, I'll starve."

This was not the whole truth. He merely wished to remind them that this horde of *zombis* was as much against his interests as theirs.

Seagrave watched the rattling truck bump its way to the road. Whenever it halted to drop one of the posse at his house, there would be a long winded exchange of gossip, and instructions for the hunt that was to be resumed in the morning. This might give Seagrave a chance to get Louise back to her home.

Venice was under arms. Oyster dredgers, hurrying from the bayous, told of the half-dead who shambled across the salt flats. Luggers had been wrecked, cabins turned inside out by the malignant prowlers from the grave.

Wind and intermittent surges of mist played tricks with all sound as Seagrave headed upstream toward the old plantation house. Drums mocked him; far off, muted mutterings. At times he thought that this was the beating of his own heart. He was worried about Louise. Again, convinced that voodoo tomtoms were beating, he paused, trying to locate the source of the sound.

Now that the posse was dispersing, the *zombi* master became bolder. There would be no unorganized search by night! Perhaps he was

He had used the drug brought from Haiti
to produce suspended animation in her.

recalling his grave-spawned ma-
rauders. There was a master.
There had to be; one living person
who commanded the dead.

A Model T wheezed past, heading upstream. It was loaded with
negroes. They were leaving the
Delta before they were shot by
mistake, or held accountable for
the ghastly doings.

WHEN Seagrave reached his
cabin, he knocked and called.
Louise answered, and came to un-
bar the door. "Those drums," she
gasped. "They have scare me. All
the time, I wait for the *zombis* to
come back."

He set the shotgun in the corner. Before he could pour himself the drink that his yelling nerves demanded, Louise was in his arms. She did not want to go home. She clung to him, and her kisses seconded her terror.

Dimly, Seagrave sensed that while she was as shaken as the rest of the natives, she was also making the most of a chance to get a permanent place in his cabin. He did not blame her; it was just the directness of her simple and primitive people.

As he wavered, she discarded subterfuge. "You 'ave been alone too long, Harry," she panted, pressing closer. "You don't do nothing but drink. You are killing yourself. Me, I will take care of you. I will not tell of the dead woman—"

She stopped short. Seagrave realized that she had been thinking of using Marilyn's apparition to corner him. That would be easy to do. If Louise told of a living corpse that prowled by night, Seagrave would be blamed for the ravages of the murderous *zombis*. There might be further outrages before the night was over.

"So that's it?" he snapped, thrusting her aside. "Go ahead and squawk!" His blood still raced, but he resented the veiled threat. "See if I care. I'll tell them myself!"

"No—that is not what I meant," she cried. "I meant—"

And then the door burst open. Seagrave's first thought was that Pierre Guérin had doubled back, searching for his missing daughter. Louise's scream corrected that before he could turn.

The black idiot was lumbering across the threshold. There was no expression in his little eyes. He had a fixed grin; it showed his long, yellow teeth. His big hands reached down to his knees. Plop—plop—plop—his bare feet, the size of shovel blades, padded over the dirt floor. His nails were caked, and stains were plain against his dark skin. Blood clotted hair was on his dirty denim jacket. And the air suddenly reeked of things long dead.

This was one of those who had pushed the earth away from their crude coffins and come forth to terrorize the living.

Seagrave leaped for his shotgun, but the shock had slowed him. He did not reach it. The monster's ham-like hand lashed out. The blow numbed Seagrave as though a sandbag had smashed over his head. He lurched over a chair, and crashed against the wall. As he recovered, clawing at the weapon, the *zombi* kicked him in the ribs.

Seagrave rolled from his knees. The contraction of his fingers set off both barrels, but the charge of shot was wasted on the wall.

Louise had recovered enough to dart toward the door. The *zombi*, however, blocked the way. He caught her with his gorilla reach. Her crimson blouse ripped. The struggle peeled her skirt loose. It wadded about her ankles and tripped her. Before she could regain her feet, the black idiot had picked her up, bodily.

She was substantial as any two frail city beauties, but in that monster's grasp, she had not a chance. He giggled, stroked her streaming hair, and ignored her frantic clawing and kicking. Seagrave, still groggy from the blow, and the kick that had cracked several ribs, made a vain effort to tackle the *zombi's* ankles.

That failed. Then an upward glimpse of Louise's flailing legs and arms, and darkness swallowed the *zombi* and his captive. Seagrave dragged himself to his feet. The room swam before his eyes. He staggered toward his hunting jacket and got a handful of cartridges. Then he picked up the shotgun, and fumbled two shells into the chamber.

His months of drinking had weakened him, though the punishment he had taken would have dazed a man in good training. But he set out after the black giant from the grave. For a few uncertain bounds, Louise's cries guided him across the misty expanse. They were heading toward the river. Then the girl's voice suddenly ceased.

Whether she had fainted from terror or had been wrenched to death, Seagrave did not know. But he carried on. Since the monster had not killed her, then and there, he told himself that there might be a chance of saving Louise.

He was no longer trying merely to avoid the wrath and suspicion of his Cajun neighbors. He could have saved himself by flight. No one in New Orleans would believe the wild yarns that circulated along the Delta. But shock and wrath were redeeming Seagrave from months of drunken remorse. A human life depended on his efforts. And Louise, despite her primitive trickery, was worth saving; which was more than he could

have said for the city friends who had abandoned him to his futile remorse.

Seagrave remembered now that he was a man. Treacherous mists made his newly aroused sense of responsibility agonizing. He stumbled on. It was useless, but he could not quit. Nor could he rout out the widely scattered natives. They would either refuse to join him by night, or they would suspect him of having a hand in the outrages.

Then the drums began mocking him. And this time, the source of them was a little more definite. While it still seemed to be an ominous muttering that came from all quarters alike, he could at times feel the deep, vibrant thump-thumpa-thump; it shook him, and the heavy air.

The *zombi,* he told himself, was dragging a victim to its master.

PRESENTLY Seagrave reached the highway. Fiddler crabs crushed under his feet. To his right was Fort Jackson, where the river curved. And now the sounds were plain; African drums made the air shudder, though they did sound louder to the ear.

Someone was chanting, inside the old parade. A wailing, sobbing, wordless rhythm; the thick lipped song of African dead. As he crept nearer, spine tingling, he caught the glow of a fire. Bare feet padded in the inclosure, but the barbican blocked his view of all but the reflected light. The crumbling drawbridge was down, as it always had been. But a few new planks were plain among the gray ones.

(Continued on page 102)

Venom Cure

"For God's sake, no!"
Lenore cried.

REEVES MALKIN thrust the bowl of warm milk beneath the glass gate that imprisoned Saprin, the Queen Cobra. He lowered the transparent panel gently, listening, while his luminous brown eyes roved over the glass fronts of other cages containing reptilian death in a hundred forms. They seemed to listen with him, those nightmare creatures coiled or stretched or

crouched in the little cellar room—moccasins and adders, copperheads and rattlers, scorpions and venomous lizards—all the poisonous crawling things the angry gods had set upon earth to hasten man's blundering march to the grave.

Their hissing mingled with the noise of the Autumn storm that swept the night-shrouded Connecticut hills and made the lonely farmhouse shudder. Then, louder

By JOHN FORD

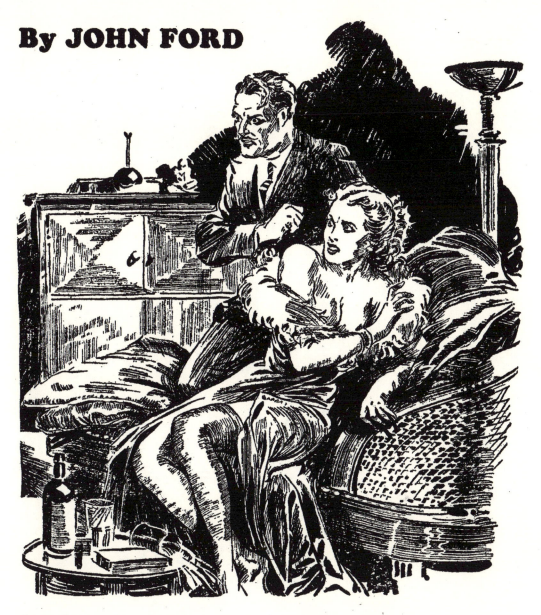

than the combined raging of the ophidian horrors and the elements, Malkin heard the muffled summons again. It was no hour, no place, no weather for callers—yet the knocker at the door was thudding violently, sending hollow echoes even into this tightly-sealed chamber beneath the earth's surface.

Malkin stood for a moment in indecision, tall and gaunt in the brilliant electric light. His face with dank black hair overhanging the high forehead, was almost cadaverous, and yet strikingly handsome. The sockets from which his eyes shone were caverns of darkness, and the shadows below his

Although the doctor was not seeking out patients, he was more than willing to see the girl who loved snakes. He understood she had venom fever—and for such illnesses he had fantastic theories. . . .

71

cheekbones were deep. He was not much over thirty, but there were deep lines about his mouth and his body was wasted, as though by consumption.

After a second of annoyed waiting, he opened a door and passed into another, larger, room equipped as a modern laboratory. He went between shelves and benches littered with test tubes and retorts and square bottles, toward a flight of steep stairs that slanted upward. He had reached the foot of the stairs when the door above opened and a woman's voice came to meet him.

"Reeves, dear—you have a patient."

He frowned up at the slim, chestnut-haired girl framed in the doorway. The light was at her back and its rays pierced the filmy wrapper she wore, silhouetting the sleek curves of her torso and hips and legs. Her body, seen thus, was beautiful and desirable, but no tenderness was reflected in Malkin's eyes or his answering words.

"You know I don't see patients any more, Leonore."

IT WAS a purely formal protest, Malkin knew that, if a patient were here, he would have no choice in the matter. He had dropped his practice a year ago to pursue, in this out-of-the way place, the weird and dangerous experiments that had first fascinated him in India, but he was still a doctor, and could not refuse to use his skill when called upon in an emergency. And this would be an emergency— an automobile accident case, perhaps, or a sudden illness with no other physician available.

"You'll want to see this patient," his young wife said. "Roy —Dr. Coleman—brought her all the way from New York for you. She has—you know, Reeves, that funny disease you wrote about in the *Medical Gazette?* The one they all laughed at?"

His face, which had darkened at the mention of Roy Coleman's name, became suddenly tense and eager.

"*Mar-ashakh?*" he asked. "The venom-fever? The—?"

Leonore laughed, almost harshly, as his feet pounded on the stairs.

"Believe it or not, Reeves, she loves snakes!"

She moved, drawing her wrapper more closely about her shapely figure, as Malkin reached her side. Her hazel eyes flashed him a look that might have been venomous in itself, and her lovely face twitched. Malkin, however, did not glance at her. He pushed past her into the living room, where the flicker of a hearth-fire was reflected in the streaming darkness of the window panes. He saw the slight girl lying on a sofa, wrapped in a coat. He turned to the stocky young man who stood with his back to the fireplace.

"What kind of trick is this, Coleman?" he demanded suspiciously.

Dr. Roy Coleman teetered on his toes. His dark, handsome face was friendly, and his lips wore a smile that curved the thin line of mustache on his upper lip. He was a younger man than Malkin, and he had all the self-assurance of youth.

"Trick?" he echoed. "Come, doctor—you never liked me, because I was a friend of Leonore, but certainly you don't think I'd try to trick you about a thing like this! The girl came to me for treatment. She'd been a snake-charmer in some two-by-four circus that folded up. She'd owned a cobra that died. She was like a dope fiend screaming for a shot in the arm, only she didn't want morphine. She wanted—venom!"

Malkin breathed: "If I could believe you—"

"I've brought the proof." Coleman nodded toward the still figure. "I gave her enough morphine to put her to sleep and brought her here as fast as I could drive. Man, it proves all the things we laughed at you for claiming! When news of it gets out, you'll be famous. If you can cure her, you'll be one of the great names in medical history—"

Malkin's lips worked. His tongue moistened them nervously. He was breathing swiftly, eagerly.

"It it's true! Her veins will be filled with antivenom. The cobra kills twenty-five thousand human beings a year in India alone. If only I can make a serum—"

COLEMAN strode to the side of the girl on the sofa. He opened the coat in which she was muffled. Malkin looked at a thin, pale face wreathed in masses of glossy black hair. Her eyes were closed, and long lashes lay across her waxen cheeks.

Leonore had tiptoed into the room. She stood close to the younger man, staring at the sleeping girl.

"Rather pretty," she murmured grudgingly, jealously.

Coleman smirked. "All pretty," he said. "Not that we doctors have much time to admire feminine charms when we're treating a case, but—" His thick fingers fumbled with the buttons at the front of the girl's blouse. He opened the garment, exposing a snow-white bosom haltered by a small brassiere, whose lacy cups were filled almost to bursting with their burden of firm-mounded flesh.

"Naida Marsh," said Coleman, pointing at a spot just below her bosom. "That's the name she used in the show business, anyway. And if you don't believe my story, Malkin—look!" He smirked again, indicating with one finger.

Naida Marsh's naked skin was like polished alabaster, flawless in texture. Her bosom stirred ever so slightly with her slow pulse and breathing. Leonore stiffened at the look in Malkin's eyes and shot a sharp glance in Coleman's direction.

Neither man, however, seemed interested in the sheer beauty of the display. Coleman's pudgy forefinger continued to point out marks on the otherwise perfect skin, and Malkin was intent on them. The marks were tiny, bluish pits—scars of bloodless wounds—and they were always in pairs. There were perhaps a dozen pairs of them, so light they hardly marred the satin smoothness of the skin.

"They are everywhere on her body," Coleman said. "On her stomach, her hips, her thighs. You may see for yourself when you wish."

Malkin exhaled a long sigh that was almost a hiss.

"Fang marks! They can't be anything else. Coleman, you say she was begging for venom?"

"Not four hours ago. She was in a dreadful state—hadn't had any for days, she said. I couldn't give it to her, of course, even if I'd known where to find it; you're the recognized venom expert in America, even though a lot of people laugh at your talk of an affinity between serpents and humans. I'd suggest you administer venom immediately in small doses — or whatever doses you see fit. It can't kill her, any more than a stiff shot of morphine could kill a hardened addict."

"I'll take her downstairs to my laboratory. No thanks, Coleman—I can carry her alone. Do you want to watch what I do? Do you, Leonore?"

Coleman shook his head. "If there's any credit to be had from this, you don't have to share it with me."

Leonore shivered, and again her oblique look of hatred flicked like the lash of a whip across her husband's face.

"Snakes!" she cried. "I've seen and heard enough about snakes to last me the rest of my life."

Obviously relieved, Malkin lifted the slim body of the girl in his arms and carried her from the room toward the cellar door. His dark eyes shone with a queer, half-mad light.

The man and woman he left behind seemed relieved, too. When they heard the door close behind Malkin, Leonore smiled crookedly.

"So you've finally done it, Roy, darling! I thought the time would never come! Every day I've felt as thought I couldn't bear it another minute, loving you and having to put up with a fool like him, shut up in this tomb with a reptile zoo. I'd have left him long ago, if we hadn't needed his money—"

"Hush!" Coleman looked uneasily toward the door through which Malkin had disappeared. "I had to be careful, dearest. We couldn't take a chance on failure. But now the fool will play right into our hands. You were right, Leonore—he's stark mad. No one will doubt it for a minute when we report what happened."

He held out his arms and she swayed against him. The filmy wrapper revealed every curve of her alluring figure as their bodies fused and their lips met in a searing kiss. . . .

"LET him who would know the divinity of Vishnu follow the Path of the Serpent. . . ."

Thus the Brahmins, repeating the laws of an ancient religion that is more than half lost to the world. Thus the lowliest Indian, gazing upon the ruins of temples raised a thousand years ago to the serpent-gods of Vishnu. Thus the devout Hindu, fearing to kill the sacred King Cobra, or his Queen, in whom the spirit of Vishnu is reincarnated.

Wisest and deadliest of beasts, worshiped since time began, destined to be feared by man until the end of things. . . .

Reeves Malkin stretched the inert form of Naida Marsh upon the low couch in the little room of the cellar, while lidless golden eyes watched through the glass of the cages. He straightened her warm

Flinging her arms wide, the girl called something in a strange tongue.

limbs, conscious of their perfection. His mind delved backward into memory.

India, blazing with unbearable sunlight, steeped in incredible darkness, with her age-old mysteries refusing to die. Young and rich, already rising to fame in medical circles, Malkin had gone there with Leonore, his exquisite and life-loving bride. She had been engaged to marry Coleman when he met her, but Coleman had been poor and an unknown, and it had been a simple matter to change her vain mind.

The interior of that fabled land had drawn him like a magnet, although Leonore would have preferred the gayer society of the English and Europeans in the port towns. The lost cities, overgrown with jungle vines, where the living serpents coiled beside the carved serpents of the temples in ambush, fascinated him. He thought he had never seen any creature more beautiful and more terrifying than the mighty cobra, with its mottled black trunk thicker than a man's arm and its membraneous hood spreading like the tremulous petals of a poison flower. He had specialized in toxicology, and he listened gravely to stories of the cobra's fatal kiss.

Only sometimes, muttered the superstitious natives, the kiss of the Queen Cobra, the female serpent, was not deadly. Sometimes a man—one chosen of Vishnu for oneness with the godhead—survived the caress of the hollow fangs. Then occurred the phenomenon known as *mar-ashakh*, the venom-fever—the *serpent-love*, they called it.

A phlegmatic British mining engineer had attempted to explain it to Malkin, over a bottle and siphon, with healthy snorts of disbelief:

"As I get it, the bally thing is like the rabies that follows the bite of a mad dog, but carried further. If a human victim of the female cobra should survive—and I, for one, doubt if that ever happened—he experiences a periodical ferment of the venom in his blood and brain. He goes mad with craving for the cobra-venom again, as a dope fiend goes mad wanting narcotics. He imagines he's a bloody snake—of all things! He does, in time, unless he can find a Queen Cobra to bite him again. And yet with each tete-a-tete with his crawling mistress, he grows more like her, until in the end he changes to a serpent and so reaches oneness with Vishnu. . . . Why are you interested in such tosh and nonsense, anyhow? Tomorrow they're having polo at Agra—"

MALKIN passed up the polo and walked out alone next day in search of the ruins of a *stupa*, a towerlike temple of great antiquity, of which he had heard. He found it in an overgrown ravine, where shadows were deep and lizards and scorpions slithered underfoot. He heard, as he came within sight of it, the thin music of the Indian flute—the instrument with which the *sappa wallahs* charm the cobra. Treading lightly, he came upon a scene that was to change and color his whole life.

A brown girl, lovely as a faun, crouched on her heels before the stone tower, coaxing a weird melody from the flute. She was nude to the waist, and from where he stood, behind her, the shape of her body and the curve of one soft breast were a vision of loveliness. But more thrilling—and awful, in its eerie implication—was the cobra that reared its hooded head high above her and swayed in a sort of sensuous paroxysm to the strains. Its ebony body writhed sinuously, its golden eyes gave forth fiery sparks, its forked tongue darted like crimson lightning between its delicate jaws.

Then the action became a hideous blur. The music shrilled to a high crescendo of madness, and broke. The girl cried something in a strange tongue and flung her arms wide. The great serpent struck; its lethal fangs penetrated the girl's golden flesh at her bosom and clung there. Girl and snake lay stretched on the ground, quivering.

Malkin raced forward, weaponless, knowing only that a human being was dying before his eyes. He threw a stone at the cobra and missed, and the monster reared back, hissing—and the girl sprang erect and faced Malkin furiously. ordering him away. The cobra struck—but she caught its lunge in the circle of her arm and pressed a spot just back of its head, and it hung over her shoulder in limp, graceful coils, with only its eyes and darting tongue seeming alive.

Malkin stared at the twin wounds in the girl's flesh, from which bright drops of blood oozed. He saw that her whole figure was pocked with the scars of similar wounds. He knew a sudden, consuming horror, and turned and fled blindly. He stumbled many times. When he reached the place where he and Leonore were staying, his clothing was tattered and he had caught a fever which kept him abed for weeks. Before he was fully recovered, Leonore had sailed with him for home.

And there the dream had grown until Malkin gave up his profitable practice and set up his laboratory in the Connecticut hills, gathering venomous serpents of every kind, determined to discover the strange power of their poison and an effective serum to combat it. For he was convinced that it was something more than an ordinary poison operating on the bloodcells, paralyzing the heart. It went beyond chemistry into realms that, in the light of present-day knowledge, might well be called supernatural.

He had written of his experiences and his belief—and fellow scientists had laughed and the newspapers had made a joke of his theory. Leonore had stormed and wept and pleaded; she could not bear the seclusion of their life, and she was certain her husband was mad. She had been slipping away to New York to see Coleman for the past year. Malkin knew it, and did not care. . . .

Malkin cared for nothing, at this moment, except the slender body of the girl stretched upon the sofa in the cellar room, and the chance it offered to carry through his experiments to their fantastic conclusion. What that conclusion must be, he already knew—but there was still a skeptical world to be convinced. At the least, the discoveries he hoped to make would show the way to an effective antidote against one not inconsiderable threat to human life; at the most, it would open vast new fields for study—physical, mental, and even spiritual fields.

"Naida," he called softly. "Wake up, Naida. Here is Saprani, the Queen Cobra. Here is the elixir you crave." He slapped her cheeks gently and chafed her wrists, but she slept on.

He opened her waist again and studied the tiny marks, some of which had already faded until they could hardly be seen. He raised her skirt, a slow inch at a time, uncovering her silk-clad knees and the tapering softness of her thighs.

(Continued on page 110)

Will O' The Wisp

FROM the lips of a drunken derelict I finally learned where Nalya Fleming, my fiancee, had hidden herself. And from this same derelict I also heard panted, incoherent mutterings that hinted at horrors I refused to believe.

Ranse Garrison was the derelict; Garrison, who once had earned ten thousand dollars a week as a character star for Altamount Productions. With the coming of sound pictures, his day had waned; toward the end, his fortune dissipated, he had become a sort of mooching ghost crawling swinishly out of Hollywood's glamorous past, living on what little he was able to borrow or beg from his more affluent friends.

Not that I was his friend; far from it! I had small use for him, even though occasionally I gave him money. Once, in his heydey, he'd had me fired without cause

By RALPH CARLE

Backward we moved under the menace of the madwoman's knife.

The surroundings in which he found the girl he loved were bizarre beyond description. But that wasn't the worst of it. He learned, without believing, that she was nourished on fresh, human blood!

from my job as assistant cameraman. Now I was a full-fledged director with a string of box-office hits to my credit—and the great Ranse Garrison was a bum. Despite the situation's irony, he came to me for charity and I gave it to him, never dreaming that one night he would reward me by telling me about Nalya. . .

I WAS annoyed at finding him ringing my doorbell that evening. For weeks I hadn't been myself. Nalya's mysterious disappearance had unnerved me; despite my own efforts and those of the private detectives I'd hired, no trace of her had been found. She had vanished utterly, along with her younger sister, Helene.

Now Garrison was staggering into my living-room, bleary-eyed, his breath reeking of rotgut. "Wha'sh it worth to you," he was mumbling, "to find out where your girl-friend'sh hiding?"

"You mean Nalya?" I cried. "My God, man, do you know anything? Speak up! Tell me!" I grabbed him by the shoulders and shook him violently.

Both fear and ratlike cunning lurked behind his drunken leer of bravado. "Hundred dollarsh before I talk. Got to have hundred dollarsh. . ." I noticed that he winced as my fingers bit into his skinny arms through the threadbare shabbiness of his topcoat.

I whipped some bills out of my wallet and thrust them into his skeletal hand. "Now, then, let's have it!" I rasped.

He counted the money; pocketed it. His sallow, desiccated face, which once had been internationally known for its ability to wear countless make-up disguises, again took on an expression of bravery that masked remembered fear— *recent* fear. "Hundred dollarsh. Tha'sh right. Cheap price you're paying for your own death." His chuckle ended in a hiccup.

"My own death—?" I said. "What the hell are you driving at? You claim you know where I can find Nalya. Now tell me before I break your filthy neck! How did you locate her, and why?"

His reddened eyes mocked me. "Don't forget her shishter used to be my wife."

That was true. At one time he'd been married to Helene. For the moment I had forgotten, just as I'd forgotten the nasty stink of the divorce. Some pretty incredible things had come out in that case; things which had helped put Garrison on the skids as far as the public was concerned.

He mumbled: "Man'sh entitled to hear from hish own wife, hunh? Wha'sh wrong with that?"

"You mean you got a message from Helene? She and Nalya are together?"

"Sure. Sure. Together with the devil. I've seen 'em. I've seen the devil. . ." He teetered on the balls of his feet. "Take my advice. Shtay away from Nalya. Unless you wanna die. . ."

I yelled: "Shut up that crazy talk! Where are they? Where is Nalya?"

"Lasht white cottage on the right in Witch Canyon back of La Crescenta. House of death . . . horror . . . shtay away . . . drink your blood . . . "

I was already sliding into my raincoat. Outside, a spring storm whiplashed the night; the wind made eerie sucking sounds around the gables of my house. Garrison's drunken mumblings about blood-drinking didn't register on my mind, at first. Then I whirled on him. "What's that?" I growled. "What did you say?"

He answered me by unbuttoning his topcoat and throwing it open. "Look!" he said.

His shirt was torn and crimson-stained. No wonder he'd winced when I grabbed his arms a moment before. His skinny shoulders and chest were welters of caked blood. The flesh showed sharp lacerations, like the marks left by an animal's fangs.

"My God!" I whispered. "How —?"

"Thank Nalya for thish . . . damn her. . ." Then his legs buckled under him. He went down, moaning incoherently.

I LEAPED over his sprawled form. A hellish thought seized me. Nalya, my Nalya of the sweet, firm breasts and coal-dark hair and lissome contours—could she have done this hideous thing to Garrison, as he claimed? If so, why? Only a maniac could have inflicted such horrible teeth-wounds. Was Nalya a madwoman? Was that her reason for dropping out of sight, hiding from the world? I'd heard of cases where persons suddenly had become afflicted with an inhuman thirst for blood. . .

Out into the drenching rain I plunged. My sedan was parked on the driveway, with Garrison's antiquated coupe blocking it. I didn't stop to think about calling for medical help for him. He was too drunk to feel pain, and his torn flesh had stopped bleeding anyhow. To hell with him; let him lie on my living-room floor and sleep off his drunken stupor. I must find Nalya and learn what was wrong. . .

I skirted Garrison's coupe by driving around it, across the lawn. Then I set out for La Crescenta, with my headlamps boring twin stabs of brilliance through the storm. Then, somehow, on Upper Foothill, I lost the way and missed the road leading into Witch Canyon. I spent thirty frantic, fruitless minutes cruising east and west before I got my bearings. Then I sent the sedan slithering and whining up the tortuous canyon way.

The narrow road came to a dead end. Storm run-off from Tujunga made a hissing, swirling creek of the canyon bed; a creek that was steadily rising with each passing moment. In fact, water was already overflowing the pavement. To my right, just beyond the end of the concrete strip, a light gleamed dimly; it came from the rear window of a white-painted cottage built against the mountainside. This must be the place, I told myself. Nalya's hiding-place. I gunned my sedan forward—

It lurched off the paving and sank hub-deep into soft muck. An eddy of water from the creek lapped up into the car proper; the engine coughed, choked and died. It would take a tow-car to get me out of that flooded place, I realized. But I wasn't thinking about that. I had only Nalya on my mind.

I strode up the muddy pathway to the white cottage. On sudden impulse I peered in through the one window from which light came. My eyes almost started from their sockets.

I was looking into the kitchen. There stood Nalya at the sink, and her hands were wet and red with blood. Fresh blood.

HER long black hair streamed gloriously down her back like a molten midnight cascade; she was wearing a nightgown of some gossamer fabric that clung like a caress to her sleek thighs, her lilting hips, her arrogant young breasts. In her dark eyes I thought I detected a peculiar glitter that shocked me almost as much as the thing she was doing.

She was holding a squirming, kicking jackrabbit on the drainboard. There was an open can of chloroform nearby, and she had saturated a wad of surgical cotton with the stuff. Now she applied the cotton to the rabbit's twitching nostrils. The animal gave a faint squeal, twitched convulsively and became quite still. But that wasn't what sent horror into my very marrow. It was something else—

That jackrabbit had been flayed alive, its skin ripped from its living body as if by tearing wolf-fangs, long before Nalya had granted it the merciful boon of death.

My mind pictured Ranse Garrison's skinny chest, bleeding and lacerated with the same sort of fang-marks...

I raced around to the front door and hammered at it. In a moment it swung open. A wizened old man peered out at me. "What do you want?" he screeched in a parchment-crackling voice that quavered with suppressed fury. Then, unexpectedly, he drew an automatic from his hip pocket and pointed it at me. "Get out, whoever you are!" he snarled. "Get away from here! We don't want visitors!"

I stared into his furtive, harried old eyes. Where had I seen him before? There was something vaguely familiar about his pudgy, pasty face; and his floury pallor seemed almost like theatrical make-up. No, I couldn't place him. But I *could* do something about that damned gun in his trembling fist.

"To hell with you!" I said savagely. "I want to see Nalya!" Then I battered his weapon aside; knocked it from his grasp. He yelped as I scooped it up and prodded him with it, forcing him backward into the house. I raised my voice. "Nalya!"

SHE came running from the kitchen; her hands, I noticed, had been washed clean of blood. "J-Jeff—!" she whimpered. "Jeff Sloane! Oh, my dear...!" Then she saw the automatic I held. "No, Jeff! For God's sake don't shoot my f-father—!"

Then I remembered him; or at least I remembered photographs of him, which Nalya had shown to me in the old days. He lived somewhere in the East, and I hadn't known that he was here in California now. As if to protect him, Nalya surged against me and wrapped her warm arms around my neck. "Jeff...!" she moaned.

There was no insanity in the way she fused her desirable body to mine. I could feel the pressure of her breasts on my chest; could smell the faint, heady fragrance of her midnight hair and see the sweet, creamy perfection of her skin through the tissue-sheer

The voice called from the distance: "Go get her! Drink her blood!"

nightgown. She was the same lovely, feminine Nalya she'd always been. My mind refused to reconcile her with that gory business in the kitchen. . . .

I shoved the automatic into my coat pocket and enfolded her in my embrace; strained her backward while I stormed kisses on her parted lips and her flawless white throat. "Nalya, honey!" I panted. "What in God's name goes on here? What's wrong? What were you doing to that jackrabbit?"

"Jackrabbit? I don't know wh-what you're talking about," she answered as the color drained from her wan cheeks. Then she said: "How did you find me? Why did you come?"

"I came because I had to know

why you disappeared without telling me," I said. "I found you through Ranse Garrison. He said he'd been here and he gave me directions—"

"Garrison?" she sucked in her breath and shot a curious glance at the old man she claimed was her father. "Why — Garrison hasn't been here, Jeff!"

That was a lie, of course; just as her denial of the jackrabbit episode was equally untrue. But I didn't press the point. I merely shrugged and said: "Why did you run away from Hollywood? What's wrong?"

"P-please don't ask questions, Jeff. I—I can't tell you anything . . . except that I just got tired of working in pictures and decided to . . . get away from it all. . . ." She gave me her lips for an ecstatic instant; then: "You must go, Jeff. Right away. You *must!*"

"Not without you. And besides, my car's bogged down now. The water's up over the road."

"Oh, God . . . !" she moaned softly.

The old man interrupted. "No help for it, Nalya. He'll have to stay the night. We can put him up in the spare room upstairs."

Nalya looked at me. "Jeff . . . if you stay . . . will you promise not to leave your room? Not to ask questions, no matter what happens?"

She was verging on hysteria; I could read it in her eyes. Perhaps madness lay behind that hysteria; I had no way of knowing. But at least I could pretend to agree; to promise anything she demanded. Later, maybe, I might learn the things I wanted to know—by ferreting through the house after everyone else was asleep. Certainly I couldn't hope to gain any information by querying Nalya or the old man. Their combined reticence had a frightened, furtive quality that puzzled and bewildered me. And I was wondering about Nalya's sister. Thus far I'd seen no evidence of her presence in the house, although Ranse Garrison had told me she was here. . . .

I WENT up to the single attic bedroom and pretended to retire. Downstairs, there were sounds of movement that eventually died as all the lights were at last turned off. There was nothing but the steady drumming of rain on the low-ceilinged roof directly above me. An hour must have passed. Then—

My door opened. Someone entered. Someone in a flowing garment of shimmery silk. At first I thought it must be Nalya, until I flared a match and saw my error. "Helene!" I whispered.

"Is—is that you, Jeff Sloane?" She glided toward me like an ethereal wraith. Before the match-flame flickered and went out, I caught a glimpse of her haggardness, and of the terror that lay in her eyes. Unlike her sister, Helene was blonde and slender—almost boyish. But her hips had a telltale flare, her legs were tapered and dainty, and her small breasts were like firm melon-halves, enticing and feminine.

I dropped the charred match—and Helen drifted into my arms. "Jeff, for God's sake get me out of this hell!" she panted. "Get me away before I go insane . . . like they are! I'll pay you any price you ask. . . ."

I held her tightly; I couldn't help doing that. It was a reflex movement, almost wholly automatic. And with the contact of her form against me, some of her fear seemed to inch into my own veins. "What's this about insanity?" I demanded in a harsh whisper. "You mean Nalya and your father—"

"My father?" she stirred bitterly. "Oh, you blind fool! That's not our father. Can't your eyes see behind make-up? That's Ranse Garrison. My former husband," she added as if the words were an epithet.

I stiffened. Garrison—! Good God, it was true that he'd been a master of disguise in his starring days. But was he still so clever that he could dupe me into not recognizing him? That was absurd. Moreover, I'd left him unconscious in my own home. How could he have got here to the canyon cottage ahead of me?

Then I remembered how I'd lost my way and wasted a good thirty minutes. He might possibly have beaten me here, while I was hunting the road. . . . But why? What was it all about? If he were Garrison, why had he lured me here?

I gave voice to the questions. Helene said: "He's Nalya's . . . lover. *And she lives on fresh blood.* It—it's horrible, Jeff. I'd rather not tell you. . . ."

"I want to know. Everything!"

"Nalya's crazy, Jeff. Crazy! Do you understand? She kills little animals . . . with her teeth! Drinks their blood! But she prefers *human* blood. It's like a dis-

ease, Jeff. It's hideous. Garrison allows her to . . . feast on him. And then he—he . . ."

My brain reeled. This was monstrous! "I don't believe you!" I almost shouted before I remembered that I must keep my tone pitched to a whisper.

"You've got to believe me—because it's true!" Helene shuddered pitiably. "They keep me locked up in my room when they have their . . . orgies. And I'm scared! Some day she'll be coming after me . . . to drink *my* blood when Garrison's veins run low . . . oh-h-h, God! How can I say these things about my own sister But it's so. . . !"

A fantastic thought struck me. "Then you believe they lured me here so that Nalya might—?"

"She wants fresh blood, Jeff. And you're big, strong, virile. Take me away! Quickly! Before it's too late!"

She was imploring me not only with her words, but with her body. She was tempting me, bribing me with the cushiony firmness of her breasts, the warmth of her curves, the softness of her skin. Her lips fluttered to my mouth in the darkness and fastened there moistly. . . .

I KNEW, then, what must be done. I had to get Helene away from that hell-damned cottage, take her back to town—and send the authorities after Nalya and Garrison. They were both insane; they must be placed in some asylum. . . . Bitterness scalded through me when I thought of Nalya in a strait-jacket, maniacally thirsting for blood. Red thirst. . . ! It was almost too demoniac to contemplate. Even worse was the thought of Nalya slaking her cannibalistic appetites on Ranse Garrison's flesh.

Helene crowded herself against me. "Take me away, Jeff! I'll be yours . . . any way you say. . . ."

I kissed her again, to soothe her. For the same reason, I stroked her bare shoulders and ran my hands over her supple young contours. Somehow my caresses seemed to arouse her. She was a woman, and I was a man, and we were both in peril. Out of the mutuality of that common jeopardy, a flame leaped into my veins. I crushed Helene to me with savage intensity. . . .

The door burst open. A flashlight glared across the room, blinding me. Helene screamed and broke free of my embrace. Then something bashed down on my head; filled my brain with a million thundering stabs of agony. The flashlight's beam broke into dancing flecks of varicolored brilliance that whirled and spun in pinwheel patterns. I sagged backward; landed on the bed. The last thing I heard was Helene's outcry—and Nalya's voice snarling: "You damned little devil."

Black unconsciousness swallowed me.

I AWAKENED with those words still ringing in my ears. Nalya had spoken them—and there had been sheer, stark fury in her tone. The fury of the mad!

I was alone in the upstairs bedroom. I pushed myself erect and fumbled for the light-switch. But when I flicked it, nothing happened. I flared a match and saw that the overhead bulb had been removed from its socket.

Footsteps sounded on the stairs outside my door.

I lay back on the bed, tense, waiting. The door opened. Nalya came toward me. I knew it was Nalya; a thin trickle of light came through the open doorway, silhouetting her nubile symmetry. I closed my eyes in pretense of unconsciousness, knowing what I must do if she were to sink her teeth into my flesh. . . .

But she didn't. She leaned over me, and her breast brushed my shoulder. I felt the softness of her lips touching my mouth; heard a whispered: "Jeff . . . darling Jeff . . ." that was like a choked sigh from some damned soul. She listened to my breathing for an instant; then she turned and left the room.

The moment she'd gone, I leaped upright; followed her silently. I heard her go downstairs; heard her voice saying: "He's . . . all right. Still unconscious, but not hurt. . . ."

"What are we going to tell him when he comes to?"

"We must make him believe it was all a dream or something," Nalya answered tremulously. "Let him think he fell out of bed and struck his head—"

"And what about Helene?"

"He mustn't know she's here. He can't guess about the cellar, surely. And she's quiet now."

From far below, a sudden outcry gave the lie to Nalya's words; a shriek that held crystalline depths of terror. That was Helene. And I went plunging down the stairs to the bungalow's main floor.

"Like hell I can't guess about your cellar!" I raged as Nalya and her companion rushed toward me. I struck out with my fists; the old man crumpled as my knuckles caromed off his chin. Nalya turned and raced to a door; jerked it open and went hurtling down a steep flight of steps.

I sprinted in pursuit. She heard me coming, and flung an agonized warning over her shoulder. "Don't follow me, Jeff—don't do it if you value your sanity! If you ever loved me—*stay where you are!*"

I paid no heed. Down those rough stairs I tumbled, to bring up short in a dimly-lighted basement where storm-water had already seeped in, so that there was at least two inches of it standing on the concrete floor.

NALYA was splashing toward the rear of the cellar. I saw her objective, and sudden sickened apprehension gripped me. Helene was strapped supine to an old table. Her nightgown was torn into pennons of ripped silk that scarcely covered her heaving breasts, her lithe body. There was a sharp butcher-knife stuck into a wooden upright nearby. I thought Nalya was heading for the knife.

I leaped after her; caught her. "Jeff — don't do anything — for God's sake—please—!" she wailed.

"You want me to stand by while you stick that knife into your sister and drink her blood?"

She wailed: "God! You don't think—you don't believe—" and tried to wrestle free of me.

I pinioned her tightly. "I can

Her hands dripped redly with fresh, warm blood.

believe only the things I see. I saw you with that rabbit in the kitchen. And I saw Ranse Garrison's bloody shoulders and chest." My eyes bored into hers. "Nalya, honey, I love you. And because I love you I've got to save you from yourself. Maybe the alienists and psychiatrists can make you forget your hellish blood-thirst. . . . Meanwhile, there's Helene."

Helene was squirming at the straps which held her flat on the table-top. "Yes, Jeff, cut me loose! Before they k-kill me!"

I held Nalya's wrists together with my left hand. With my right, I grasped at the knife sticking into the wooden upright—

A voice said: "Drop it!"

I froze. The old man whom Nalya called her father was coming down the stairs. He was aiming his automatic at me. He must have taken it out of my pocket while I lay unconscious a while ago.

"Put down that gun, Garrison," I told him. "You can't get away with this."

"Garrison. . . ? You call me Garrison? You must be mad, sir. As mad as my poor Helene. . . . Stay away from that knife, I tell you! I know what you're up to. You want to cut Helene free. Hasn't there been enough blood-letting for one night, you fool?"

I started to answer. A knocking upstairs stopped me. He handed his automatic to Nalya. "Stand guard while I see who that is," he said. I noticed that there was nothing drunken nor senile in the way he dashed up the steep steps.

Helene moaned: "Do something for me, Jeff . . . dear God, don't let them murder us both! I'm afraid. *Afraid!*"

I turned to Nalya. "Give me the gun, my dearest. You know you wouldn't shoot me with it anyhow."

Her eyes were moist. "If only you could understand . . . but it's too horrible . . . *Jeff!*" Her voice rose keeningly as I snatched the automatic away from her. Maddened fear scrawled itself in her suddenly-widened eyes. "Jeff — don't do anything! Not until I've explained! *You're loosing hell itself, Jeff, if you—*"

SHE sprang at me like a maniac. Hating myself, I struck her; sent her sprawling in the water. She mewed like a whipped kitten. I grabbed the knife from the upright and slashed Helene's bonds. "Help me with Nalya!" I grated.

"Yes. Of course. We must do something for her," Helene answered in a tiny, choked voice that held a sobbing background. "But first I must have strength. . . ." And without warning she flurried into me. Her long fingers ripped my coat open, tore my shirt. Like a cobra striking, her head shot downward *and I felt her sharp teeth meeting in the flesh of my shoulder!*

I dropped both gun and knife. For an instant I stood petrified by this nightmare-thing that was happening to me. Then I seized Helene's shoulders; thrust her away. Her mouth dripped red with blood. My blood. . . !

Nalya struggled to her knees. "I tried to warn you, Jeff!" she gasped frantically. "Now you know why I sent for my father, why we took this cottage, why I dropped out of sight. It was to keep Helene here, out of the insane asylum . . . or worse! She's mad; blood-mad! She kills animals . . . skins them with her teeth . . . drinks their blood before they're dead. . . . I was putting one of her rabbits out of its misery when you saw me in the kitchen. . . ."

Then I realized the truth. *Helene* was the maniac, not Nalya. Helene, who had fooled me with her story, up in the bedroom. And now she had picked up the knife I'd dropped. She was coming at me. "Nice, big Jeff! I'll cut you just a little bit. Not enough to hurt you much. You won't miss the blood I take. Big, strong Jeff. . . ."

As if in some fantastic dream, I backed away. My arm went around Nalya's cuddly waist. Both Nalya and I were in jeopardy now. That knife in the madwoman's fist might just as well pierce Nalya's heart as my own. I cursed myself for having dropped the automatic; there was no chance of finding it now; under three or four inches of rising water. Even if I found it, I'd not be able to use it, probably. It was wet. And how could I bring myself to shoot Nalya's sister in any case?

"God!" I whispered.

Nalya said: "I'll try to hold her off. You make a break for the stairs, Jeff. This is my problem, not yours."

"Leave you here alone with . . . her? Never!" I grated. Helene was stalking us and licking her red-smeared mouth. We were backing away from her, around and around the cellar; the scene was a nightmare out of hell itself. "The man upstairs — he *is* your father?" I panted.

"Yes. Who else. . . ?"

"Helene tried to make me believe it was Ranse Garrison in make-up."

NALYA shivered against me. Always we moved backward, away from the menace of the madwoman's knife. "Garrison!" Nalya cried. "He's the one who's responsible for all this! While he was married to Helene he did things . . . that wrecked her mind and made her what she is now! He taught her to drink blood, damn him! Only I never knew about it until long after the divorce . . . when I caught her with her pet poodle . . . her teeth in its throat . . . that's when I rented this bungalow and brought her here. . . ."

Swish! The knife slashed at us like a live thing. I warded it off. Helene grinned and stalked us again. Nalya moaned: "Then, today, Garrison showed up here. I don't know how he found us—"

"I sent him a note and asked him to come and take me away," Helene broke in. "You were surprised to see him, weren't you, sister dear?"

Nalya sobbed. She turned to me. "When he came, he undid all the good we'd accomplished. Helene hadn't . . . been thirsty . . . for almost a week. But when she saw Garrison she tore at him. . . ."

"That explains the marks on him when he came to my house!" I said. "But why did he send me here instead of notifying the authorities?"

I got my answer from the stairway — in Ranse Garrison's own voice. He was crouching there, grinning down at us all. "I sent you here because I want money!" he chortled. "Once Helene kills you, I can blackmail Nalya and her father with the knowledge.

(Continued on page 109)

Maiden of Moonlight

[Continued from page 17]

And because the Indian girl was there. . . . The idea kept occurring to him that she must have been there all those years—yet she wasn't more than twenty, twenty-two or three at the most.

To hell with such thoughts. "We'll have a party, baby," he said to the blonde.

"Sure we will!" She put her arm around him as they went up the stairs. He could smell the heavy perfume that she wore. He could feel the soft, lush curves of her body.

THERE was a bed and a couple of chairs in the room. A tiny kitchenette held a refrigerator from which the girl took ice and liquor. She made them both drinks, stiff ones. "Here's to a good time," she said.

He had the crazy idea that something was going to happen to the whiskey before he could drink it and he gulped it fast. She said, "You did need a drink, didn't you, mister. Here, I'll make you another."

"Let me pay for it."

She laughed. "You don't need to pay for the whiskey. I'm giving you that."

"I want to."

"Aw no."

"Well, I'll make it up to you later. I'll pay you plenty." He was reaching for the money, but she handed him the drink and he left the money in his pocket for the time being. Deep inside him there was a foolish fear that if he tried to pay now something might happen. And he didn't want anything to happen. The blood was pounding through his veins.

The blonde said, "We're going to make a real party of it, mister. I'll get comfortable."

She played modest. She stepped back of a screen. From behind it she said, "You look like you been out in the country recently. That where you made that wad of money?"

"Sure," Charlie said. "I been prospecting."

She said, "Well, you had better luck than one fellow I met about a year ago."

Charlie was making himself another drink. In his empty stomach the whiskey seemed to catch fire and burn with a dull roaring sound. It ran hot through his veins. He said, "What happened to him?"

"He was nuts. I met him one night and at first I thought he was just drunk. But he was crazy. He kept talking about some Indian girl that ran around naked guarding a batch of money—or helping some old man guard it, or something."

Charlie emptied his drink without tasting it. He was suddenly cold all the way through his body, cold into the marrow of his bones. He took a fourth drink, straight. "Talking about—what . . . ?"

The blonde came out from behind the curtain. She wore a black silk dressing robe now, and apparently that was all. It was tied tight at the waist, but fell open above and below. When she moved, he could see the trembling of her round white breasts and the flash of smooth legs. "How do you like me?"

He wanted to take her in his arms, crush her against him, put a fierce struggling end to the deep ache in his body. But he heard himself saying, "What did he tell you about—the Indian?"

"Aw he was just crazy." She took her glass in one hand, put the other arm around Charlie and led him over to the couch. When he sat down, she sat on his lap. "This fellow kept talking about her being a ghost or something. Seems like a long time ago the white men done her wrong; killed her family and stole their land and got the gold off it, and sort of made her into a slave until she died. Now she's put a curse on the money that was made from her tribe's land and nobody can spend it. And she makes white men kill each other for it, because she hates 'em. The guy was nuts."

"What happened to him?"

"That was the funny thing. He kept saying he was going back, saying he had to kill some old man to get the girl. And about a week later I see in the paper where he was found dead out on the mountain. Some rocks had fell on him."

The liquor was roaring in Charlie's head. It made words like the Indian girl's voice: *Because I like for white men to kill. . . . He's old, but he's clever. He's killed them all because he knew they had to come back and had traps for them. . . .*

THE blonde emptied her glass. She moved in Charlie's arms, leaning back and raising her face so that she looked up at him, waiting to be kissed.

Then her own face seemed to freeze with terror. Her eyes bulged. She leaped up and began to back away from him. "What—what's wrong with you?"

"Nothing. Drunk maybe. Maybe I've got to go back out there too. But first . . ."

He reached for her. She cried, "Keep away from me! You—You—I'm scared of you!"

"Don't be!" He clutched at her. He caught the robe, ripped it as she tore away. She hadn't worried about it before, but now she tried to cover herself from his wild, hot eyes. "I'll pay you!" he said. "I'll pay you all you want!"

"Get out of here! I'm scared of you!"

"I'll pay! A hundred dollars! A thousand!"

"Get out! Please. . . . Please. . . ."

As he rushed at her she began to scream. . . .

HE COULDN'T remember much after that. Running from the police, dodging, hiding, crawling through dark alleys that whirled and spun drunkenly across the night. But gradually he made his way back toward his car and when he had found it he knew what he was going to do—what he had to do.

He was going back. He had not eaten in more than thirty hours, but it was not food that he wanted, or liquor either. His uncle might be waiting, with the traps that had killed other men. But Charlie would take his chance on dodging them. He had ten thousand dollars in his pocket and he wasn't going to throw it away. If he couldn't spend it, he would go back and find out why. And he would see the Indian girl that he had seen only once by moonlight. This time she wouldn't get away from him. . . .

POLICE found his car where it had given out of gas. And a week later two hunters saw circling buzzards and found the body of a man who had evidently fallen from a high cliff. There was no money in his pockets.

Prayer to Satan

[Continued from page 29]

ing, "Something knocked me silly. That Laylat—Lilith's daughter—God, what a nightmare—"

Then he saw the horse. It was Saoud's mount. Painfully, he pulled himself into the saddle. He could not make much better time than on foot, but riding would save his strength. For a moment, he was not sure whether he should ride on: better to go back and find the Black Book, and tell Khosru Khan what had happened. But he ended by discarding that idea; the first thing to do was to get those fools on the road. Once they saw him they would believe, they would realize their danger, they would know that not even his friendship with the *khan* could save them from the penalty for entering the forbidden shrine. They were not worth it, but his obligation drove him; they were under his protection.

He rode on. The moon was setting, but Saoud's horse knew the way to camp. The false dawn lightened the gloom for a little while, and then came blackness like that of the pit where he had faced a

force which he now attributed to senses torn awry by the shock of bullets and the fall against jagged rock.

FINALLY he could distinguish the camp. There was a light still burning in his tent. He slid from the saddle, reeled dizzily. A wave of wrath shook him. He stood there, looking at the shadows cast on the canvas. Diane and Howarth were wasting no time. They were not in the least concerned about his possible return.

That was what whipped his fury, and restored his flagging strength. He strode toward the tent, and jerked the fly aside. They were too engrossed to hear him.

Diane was stretched out in a collapsible lounging chair. Her sea green robe trailed away from her body, and the light reached through the frail gown which clung to bosom and leg.

"Darling," she said to Howarth, "maybe we should leave, regardless. Even though those fools couldn't find the book, even though Khosru's people do find it, and him, they may blame us."

Howarth looked at his watch. "My God, I didn't know it was so late!"

He turned toward the door. Diane exclaimed, "How did that get opened?"

Neither saw Mason. The shock of full understanding had made him recoil, so that the light from the doorway no longer reached him. He knew now that they had not expected him back; that Howarth, humiliated by that beating, had sent some of the Arabs to intercept him, to recover the Black Book. They must have come back, saying that they had found him and Saoud, but not the sacred volume. "Maybe," Mason told himself, "they don't realize the Arabs shot us."

But he could not convince himself. They were too pleased with everything; they had sent men to kill him, get the Black Book.

And then he felt the earth shake, and heard the drumming of hoofs. Spurts of flame lashed the darkness. There were yells, screams from the Arab camp. Brett came bounding from his tent. Diane shrieked, leaped to her feet. Bearded men with high peaked turbans closed in on all sides, Howarth, running to get his pistol, spun and doubled up; a curved blade slashed, and Brett fell.

Then Khosru Khan caught Diane by the shoulder, tearing her robe from her, ripping her gown to the waist. "O daughter of murder!" he roared, "whether he lives or dies, he will not save your skin!"

During all this whirlpool of fury, Mason had said not a word, had not made a move; things were happening too rapidly, and his senses were spinning. As he stared, new horror thrusting aside the old, the entire scene blurred. The sounds came as from a great distance, and blackness gulped him up.

WHEN he could again perceive what was about him, the sun was shining. He was stretched out on a scarlet Kurdish rug in Khosru Khan's reception room. It was cool in that thick-walled fortress, and the sounds of the town were well shut out. His first thought was that he was a captive, the only survivor of the massacre; then he realized that he was not shackled, and that there were no guards about him.

He made an effort, a painful effort, and sat up. A girl was kneeling beside him, and at his first move, she set embroidered cushions to support him.

She wore a red velvet hood with silver filigree, and long pendants that caressed her cheeks. Her velvet jacket had a high collar; a long tunic concealed her figure, but Mason shut his eyes, and remembered every exquisite curve of that lovely body.

He remembered: for this was Laylat, the daughter of Lilith, with long black hair and wide dark eyes. And when she smiled, he had no remaining doubt. More than that, there was something in her eyes, something playing about the corners of her mouth which told him that he and this lovely creature had met before, had wandered in that mysterious borderland between life and death.

"What has happened?" he asked. "And who are you?"

"I am Layla, the *Khan's* daughter," she answered; and the voice was as familiar as the name. "We found you in the valley, wounded and unconscious, and your servant also. We found the sacred book in the crevice of a rock. Arab thieves must have taken it, and when they met you, they must have mistaken you for one of us, and shot you and your servant. Or so my father says, for I was asleep when all that happened."

"How long have I been here?"

"It is two days now. And I have been praying for you, begging for your life." She clapped her hands, and when a servant entered, she said, "Tell my father that our friend is awake and well."

Outside, a beggar whined for alms. Mason asked, "Is that the blind man by the well?"

Layla nodded.

"Give him a piece of silver, for me, and tell him that his prayer to the Lord Peacock was answered."

Layla's face did not change, but he thought he saw a flash of understanding in her eyes. She rose, and went to the door. By now, Mason was sure that he had left no footprints in the shrine of the peacock, and that the daughter of Lilith had left no traces; yet he was equally certain that he and the *khan's* daughter had faced the Presence together.

Khosru Khan stepped into the great hall, and greeted his guest. "I have heard that Arabs from the river raided your camp, leaving none alive. And now that no duty takes you away, stay here and be one of us."

Mason looked for a moment at the slender figure silhouetted against the arched doorway; Layla was handing the blind beggar a coin. Then Mason said, "My blindness was greater than his, and he gave me the gift of sight. Ever since I left here, I have seen what I had not seen before."

The *khan* stroked his beard and smiled a little. "But Layla had seen you before, and now she is glad."

The Caverns of Time

[Continued from page 41]

spines capable of tearing a man's flesh from his body in great ragged bites!

The whip uncoiled. With the speed of light it leaped across the room, whistling its challenge. Grayson threw up his arms to protect his face: a gesture so tardy that it wrung a peal of laughter from his tormentor.

"Dance, Grayson!"

But Grayson did not dance. Inch by inch he gave ground, while the gleaming whip menaced him. Judie, pale and lovely in the gown that hid none of her exquisite beauty, watched through a mist of anguish. Sarah Jules crouched like a toad upon the pit steps. Inexorably the silver serpent drove Grayson into a corner from which there could be no escape.

He flung himself forward, risking the bite of the lash in a desperate attempt to reach his tormentor. But the metal was swifter. Coiling about him, it made rags of his clothes, laying bare his skin. He fell back and it pursued him.

Blood reddened the rags of his clothing. Sweat oiled his face. No more could he retreat. And still the Master advanced.

"This, Grayson," Nicholas taunted, "is but a sample of what awaits you in the Pit. Your bride can tell you of that, for her father was the last to die there. Like you, Grayson, Carlton Clough was an outsider. He took himself a wife. He attempted to depart to the Outside, with his wife and child. He paid, Grayson, and his wife died of madness in the caverns, seeking him. His daughter—your bride—can tell you, Grayson!"

Grayson's endurance died. Bloody beyond recognition, he sank to the floor and lay unmoving. The whip licked out once more to test him; then the Master drew closer, his gaze evil, while Sarah Jules chuckled malignantly on the stone steps and the girl Judie sobbed her heart out.

"Not dead, I think," Nicholas murmured, bending closer. "You see, Sarah, he breathes. I was very careful not to—"

SWIFT as light, Grayson's hand closed over the silver snake. With all his strengtth he reared up!

It played no favorites, that nendish serpent! It's frightful barbs bit deep into the Master's throat, and then Grayson was on him, battering him with crimson fists. With the whip wound like a noose about his neck, Nicholas fought back. But Grayson scarce felt his blows. The sight of Judie's trembling body, the dark knowledge of what she had been through, gave Grayson a madman's strength.

The withered woman clawed at his legs, to upset him, and he sent her tumbling down the steps with a kick that silenced her. On the brink of the steps the Master tottered, striving to free his throat from the serpent's deadly embrace.

Grayson measured him. One more blow would finish him. But it was not needed. The giant toppled. The silver serpent, his own grim weapon, was the end of him. For as he fell, the tail of the whip fastened under the body of Sarah Jules, drawing taut with one grisly wrench the barbed loop that encircled the Master's throat.

Sobbing a little, Grayson took his bride in his arms, feeling the warmth of her against him, the beating of her heart beneath a soft, round breast. He put his coat about her. His mouth found hers, and for a moment nothing else mattered except the seeking velvet softness of her lips, the quivering of satin-smooth curves beneath his hot hands.

Then they fled. The ghosts of silent houses disappeared behind them. The valley slept.

Strange, Grayson mused, that here in this ancient, evil place he had found himself a wife, a girl more beautiful in body and spirit than any he had met in his own so-called civilization. Joy filled his heart, despite the agonies inflicted by the silver whip. "You are sure of the way, darling?" he muttered.

"Almost," she said, "I found it before. I can reach the place where Sarah Jules trapped me. If you know the way from there . . ."

Grayson nodded. How many hours ago was that? Centuries, it seemed! Time meant nothing here. "How does it feel to be Mrs. Grayson?" he asked, holding her hand.

"I love it." She smiled shyly. "That is—I think I will, darling."

"What he said about your father —is it true?"

"Yes, Grayson."

"But your father can't be dead! Indirectly it was he who sent me to this place!"

"That I do not understand," she said. "He died in the Pit, many years ago."

Grayson was too weary to let it trouble him. He saved his strength for walking, for now they were through the valley and climbing. It would be a long, difficult climb.

Twice he stopped to rest, sinking wearily into the snow. His legs had grown numb with cold, and he felt the loss of so much blood. Back in the Master's house, in a red pool on the floor, lay the strength he now so sorely needed.

It was during one of these rest periods, while he lay with his head cradled on Judie's warm lap, her body warming his, that he heard the first sounds of pursuit. The wind brought them—faint, far-off echoes of shouting in the valley below.

Grayson sat up with a start. "They're after us!"

With Judie's help he struggled on. But now she almost had to carry him. Time and again he stumbled. The snow stung his wounds. The wind iced his blood.

AUDIBLE now without intermission were the sounds of pursuit, steadily creeping closer. Looking back, Grayson saw lights in the windy dark below. High out of the valley they had climbed, but steeper still loomed the ascent ahead.

"This," Judie gasped at his side, "is where I was turned back before. I know not the way from here. Only Sarah Jules has ever gone the whole way Outside!"

The lights were gaining. Grayson stumbled on. He fell and crawled, with Judie's low, pleading voice beating against the mass of pain that was his mind. At last he could stand no more.

"Go on without me," he muttered. "Alone, you'll have a chance."

Judie's tears wet his face as she shook her head. "If it's a trail they follow," she cried, "then a trail I'll give them! I'll lead them away from you!"

"No!"

She knelt beside him, looking deep into his eyes as though in one brief fragment of time she sought to etch the image of him on her memory forever. Sobbing, she parted her coat and drew his face against her, and clung to him. The warmth of her was a delicious drug. The satin sweetness of her skin was a caress. Her lips found his, desperately, and her slender body was a flame against his own.

"Try to go on," she whispered. "If I lose them, I will find you. If not . . . there will be another day, my darling." From her wrist she slipped a bracelet, a chain of gold which Grayson had last seen in the caverns, when it linked the two of them as man and wife. It closed over his own wrist, and she was gone.

Too weak to cry out, he saw her speeding down the darkness, obliterating their prints as she went. Then she fled from the path and vanished.

Grayson dragged himself on. The shouts of the pursuers died into a silence that reared behind him like a barrier. The cold crept through him. Only the dim hope that his bride might escape, and somehow return to him, kept him going.

How long he crawled he did not know. When he collapsed at last, he continued to crawl through a nightmare, pursued by shadows that gave him no rest.

HE THOUGHT at first, when he waked, that the face above him was her face, but it had no answering smile for him and was quickly replaced by a man's.

"Grayson, by God! You're out of it at last!"

Grayson stared about him—at the bed, the hospital room, the nurses. "How long?" he muttered. "How long have I been here?"

"Days. You've had a tough time of it, old man. Chap who picked you up was a farmer out clearing the road after the storm. He got my name from papers in your wallet, and notified me. Your car was found in a shed not far from where you keeled over."

Grayson reared on his elbows, his eyes burning with a strange

fever. "What shed, Ted? Where?"

"Back of an old store, on the road from Appalachia. That is, it used to be a store. Been abandoned for years, I'd say."

A frown crossed Grayson's gaunt face. "Abandoned?"

"Yes. Whatever possessed you to invade this neck of the woods anyway?"

"Your telegram."

"Telegram? I didn't send you any telegram."

"But you did. In my clothes—you'll find it somewhere—"

"Everything that was in your pockets is right here. No telegram, Grayson."

"A man named Carlton Clough," Grayson began, his voice shaken with sudden doubt. "You wired that he—"

"Who?"

But Grayson's gaze had fallen on the little pile of his possessions that lay on the table. Weakly he reached toward it, drawn by something that gleamed yellowly in the room's dim light.

"Who?" the man beside the bed asked again. "Carlton *Who?*"

"It doesn't matter," Grayson whispered. Gone from his voice was the shadow of doubt that had made it so nearly inaudible. In his eyes again flowed that strange ecstatic fever. In his hand lay a golden chain, the bridal link placed upon his wrist by the beautiful girl he loved.

He stared at it, seeing again the glorious beauty of her slim white body, feeling again, ecstatically, the sweet, thrilling warmth of her.

"Wait for me, darling," he whispered. "Wait for me, Judie! I'm coming!"

Payment in Blood

[Continued from page 57]

he!" he raged. "You must have been listening outside my door when Lynne came to me. You captured her when she went out. Then you took her place and brought me out here to trick me into touching that live fence!" His fist lashed out to catch her on the jaw. She landed in the undergrowth, skirts flurrying. She lay still.

HE TURNED and pelted for the house. Lynne was there. Lynne —alive, though she'd claimed to be dead. Lynne, held in some foul thrall that had caused her to lie. . .

He reached the open front door and arrowed through. He heard a whimpering moan. Lynne's moan. It came from somewhere below—in the cellar. Was her father torturing her? "God!" Greyling said. And, finding the cellar staircase, he launched himself downward.

He had enough presence of mind to be silent in his descent. As he entered the brilliant light-glare of the cellar, he blinked and was almost blinded. Then his marrow seemed to be changed to slimy horror.

At the far end of the chamber, beyond the furnaces and crucibles, there was a cot. Lynne cowered on it, her eyes wide with terror. Her silken robe was torn to ribboned tatters, half baring her vibrant young body. The sleek length of her creamy thighs gleamed like ivory in the strong light. Over her leaned that hideous black man whom Greyling had seen upstairs earlier in the evening. The black's slobbery, blubbery lips were drawing close to Lynne's averted mouth. His apish fingers were opening and closing spasmodically as they reached inexorably for her shrinking body. . . .

Watching this scene, with his back toward Greyling, stood a tall, gaunt figure who spoke in a snarling maniac rasp: "You sent him a letter. *What did you tell him?* How did you get the letter posted?"

"No—no! I swear I never wrote to Dirk! Not—not since a year ago —a year ago this very week!"

Dirk Greyling stiffened. A year ago . . . ? And the letter had lain in his house unopened, unanswered, while he made his lonely tour of the world? They why had he thought it was mailed just a few days ago?

The answer dawned on him. He had correctly read the date, but had mis-read the postmarked year.

What had happened in the interim? What foul, hellish things had been going on here on this island mountain since Lynne sent that invitation?

The tall, gaunt figure spoke again. "Unless you tell me, you know what will happen. Sambo's been waiting a long time for this moment. . . . What information did you write to Dirk Greyling? Not that it matters, he's dead by now. Molly took him to the fence; he's fried to a crisp by this time. *But I must know!*"

"Oh God—please—!"

THE huge black reached for her suddenly, lifted her in his arms. She shrieked madly as her face neared his leering countenance. She clawed at him desperately and her slim white legs flailed madly, in a futile effort to escape. And then Greyling leaped.

He bashed into the tall, gaunt man; knocked him sprawling. Greyling caught one look at the fellow's features as he charged past. *"Jeb Farrand, the taxi-man!"* he panted. Then he came to grips with the coal-black Sambo.

The negroid giant d r o p p e d Lynne to the floor where she huddled, terror-stricken, a pathetic tangle of torn silk and sprawling, bare legs and arms. The black whirled around, thick lips peeled back from blue, toothless gums. He flicked out a razor, snapped it open, slashed at Greyling's throat.

Greyling warded off the blow with an upflung arm; felt the blade biting into flesh and bone. He exploded a savage punch to his antagonist's jaw. The black merely blinked and closed in, unhurt. Greyling pumped vicious fists into the giant's soft guts. They told. The black doubled over, wheezing and mumbling. Greyling saw a heavy wrench on the workbench alongside him. He grabbed it, hurled it—

The chilled-steel tool smashed full into the black's forehead; split skin and skull with a sickening sound. The giant went down with his blood-smeared brains oozing from that hideous crevice in his forehead; he was dead before he fell.

Greyling heard a hoarse shout: "Dirk—look out—behind you!"

He whirled. For the first time he saw Professor Linwold trussed to a chair over in a far corner. It was Linwold who had yelled that warning. Jeb Farrand was getting to his feet, moving forward with murder in his glare.

"Hold it!" Greyling panted. "Stand where you are or I'll break you in half! You're the one behind all this night's work! After you left me at the gate, you must have driven around to another entrance into the grounds, on the other side of the mountain. You forced Linwold to invite me in; forced him to say over the phone that the current was off. You wanted me killed. *Why?"*

The old professor answered. "It was that newspaper article about my making diamonds. . . . " he gasped weakly. "Farrand believed the stones could be manufactured commercially. He walked in on me six months ago; brought Molly Madden and that black man with him. I was made prisoner. They captured Lynne. They . . . they held her here in the cellar; threatened to let the negro attack her unless I obeyed orders. . . ."

"God!" Greyling choked. "Then it was Farrand who put up that electrified fence to keep intruders out! Farrand who circulated the report that Lynne was dead. He used her as a whip over you—to force you to carry on your experiments for his profit!"

"Y-yes. . . ."

THEN the fake taxi-driver grinned. "Ye got the straight of it, mister. But ye'll never git out of here with your information. Sure I lied an' tried to scare ye away—until ye said ye'd had a letter from the old man. That's why I knew I had to kill ye; I thought mebbe the letter had told ye too much. Ye got by the gate, damn ye. Ye got past every trap I set for ye. An' ye tumbled to the truth when Lynne managed to sneak past Sambo an' come to your room. But now you're finished." He drew an automatic from his pocket and aimed it at Greyling's heart.

From the floor, Lynne snatched up the wrench that had killed the black. She struck at Farrand's gun-wrist, deflected his aim. It was the chance Greyling wanted. He battered into Farrand, smashed him backward under a flurrying avalanche of maddened punches. Farrand lost his balance—

Lost his balance, and fell through the open door of that huge crucible in which Lynne Linwold was falsely reported to have died; whose current was now disconnected, so that the interior no longer held heat.

Greyling saw him tumble into the aperture. And he slammed the door. "That'll hold you until we get the police up here!"

A new voice shrieked: "That's what you think, sucker!" Greyling pivoted—to see the brunette Madden woman hurtling at him like a tigress.

He side-stepped her. She caromed into the wall. Her elbow brushed a huge rheostat. From within the crucible, Farrand screamed horribly. A red hell-glow was burgeoning within his prison. He battered at the thick glass, trying to smash his way out. The glow grew whiter, more incandescent. And as Greyling watched in horror, he saw Jeb Farrand being roasted alive. . . .

"That makes you a murderess," he said to the brunette girl.

She slumped in a dead faint at the sheer horror of the thing she had done.

Then Greyling released Professor Linwold; took Lynne into his arms. They were slaves of Farrand's avaricious cruelty no longer. They were free. Six months of agonized hell had, for them, ended.

And for Dirk Greyling and Lynne Linwold, it was the beginning of happiness.

Haiti Magic

[Continued from page 69]

Water hyacinths hid the stagnant muck of the moat. Poisonous moccasins, inert at night, lurked among the lily pads. But something worse was inside the abandoned fort.

If he could get the master, the *zombis* would be harmless. Bits of forgotten lore told him that. Seagrave crept over the drawbridge. He began to recognize words of the chant; Haitian patois, French even more debased than that of the Delta natives. Haiti, the home of voodoo, had sent this curse.

He passed through the barbican's shadowy mass. Another and shorter drawbridge separated him from the central inclosure. Half a dozen negroes capered about the fire. Others beat drums and shook rattles, chanting as they played. There was no sign of the monster who had captured Louise. Seagrave was puzzled; this was not the human sacrificial ritual he had expected.

Bottles of gin, some emptied, some full, dotted the flagstones.

The dark tunnel that opened from Seagrave's left connected with each of the casements of the hexagonal fort. By following it, one could make a circuit of the inclosure, passing by powder magazines, gun embrasures, storerooms. He crept into the black shadows. That infernal drumming blotted out all sounds; it likewise muffled his own heavy breathing, and uncertain footsteps.

A spindle of white wavered in the darkness just ahead. It had an eerie glow that outlined a slender, feminine shape. As Seagrave recoiled, breath sucking in through suddenly clenched teeth, a woman's voice mocked him: "You're surprised, aren't you, Harry?"

Marilyn was speaking. Seagrave shrank against the wall. Strong hands caught his arms. The gun was snatched from his grasp. Then lanterns were unmasked, and a man with a swarthy face and black moustaches came out of a casemate.

Whatever made the woman's body phosphorescent was not strong enough to produce a glow in the yellow light. It was Marilyn, blonde and lovely; her slim legs and shapely torso smiled through the transparent shroud. But she was breathing, smiling. Her eyes gleamed mockingly. This was no corpse; and the dark man was José Castro, the admirer who had fled.

The two burly negroes dragged Seagrave into the casemate. The chanting had ceased. Others of the crew came in. The only escape was through the gun embrasure, and into the moccasin infested moat below. Castro said, "She never was dead. But in Haiti and Santo Domingo, we know the secrets of Africa. Some potions produce a temporary death, and whoever recovers becomes a *zombi*, one of the living dead."

He smiled at Seagrave's shudder, and went on. "Another infusion of herbs produces catalepsy, but the recovery leaves no per-

When answering advertisements please mention SPICY MYSTERY STORIES

manent effect. This was what your wife took. To keep you from killing her and me."

"Wasn't it simple?" Marilyn mocked. "You thought I'd stay in that crypt. But I didn't. We went to Haiti, José and I. But now we're back."

"Why?" Seagrave croaked. "You were safe, you two!"

Castro laughed. "Among other things, to make you a *zombi*. A real one. Like those who roam about the Delta. You, and that Cajun girl."

José Castro's voice was level. His dark eyes had no gleam of madness. This was no maniac's whim. Seagrave remembered a snatch of the Haitian criminal code. It forbade, under penalty of death, the administering of drugs of the sort this renegade had mentioned. However else *zombis* might be produced by African necromancy, there was a direct method by which the living were poisoned; and this was what Seagrave faced.

"But why Louise?" he croaked.

"I'd tell you," answered Castro. "But you wouldn't remember."

Another negro came in with a steaming kettle and a dipper. The others closed in, lifting Seagrave from his feet. Despite his struggles, they placed him on the table. "Tie him," Castro commanded, "and hold his nose. He'll drink enough of it to do the trick!"

BUT a scream from somewhere in the depths of the tunnel made Castro and his helpers start. There was a bestial growl, the screech of nails pulled out of wood, the splintering of boards. Mari-lyn cried, "Picot's loose! He'll kill her!"

Castro darted into the corner and picked up a heavy whip. Its lashes were tipped with ten-penny nails. He growled, "I'll teach that half witted ape to fool around!"

Despite the efforts of the four who held him, Seagrave sat up for a moment. Picot, the prowling monster, had Louise in his arms. He was shambling down the passageway. For a moment his black bulk blocked the archway. His frantic captive clawed and kicked. He had broken out of his cage and gone back to the victim he had been forced to abandon.

The whip hissed. Seagrave could no longer see, but he heard the lash smack home, and the groan of the gigantic half wit. He knew now that Picot was no *zombi*, else a scourge would not be needed to subdue him.

Another blow. Louise had ceased screaming. Then Castro yelled. The blacks who held Seagrave jabbered. In the excitement, they relaxed their grasp. The captive made a sudden wrench and rolled off the table.

Marilyn cried a warning. But Seagrave had picked up the steaming pot of herbs. He hurled it squarely at the two who tried to recapture him. They howled as the scalding liquid drenched their faces and bodies.

The others lost their chance to nail Seagrave. As he recovered the emptied pot, Picot came into the compartment. He was snarling, flailing his abnormally long arms. Two of the crew raced toward the gun embrasure to dive into the moat. This half wit, tasting blood early that evening, was no longer to be browbeaten by his master.

He had dropped Louise, but Marilyn looked just as good to him. He caught her. She might have been a doll, for all the effect her weight had on his gorilla strength. Her voice cracked at the end of a shrill scream. Before Seagrave, horrified at seeing that monster with a woman in his arms, could crash down on his bullet skull with the pot, Picot and his victim were in the passageway.

Castro, brushing blood from his face, staggered into view. He no longer had his scourge; only the broken handle. Seagrave, startled, smacked down with both hands. The heavy pot flattened the renegade doctor to the floor. Bones crunched under the impact.

A shotgun roared. Picot howled. Seagrave could not see him in the gloom of the passage, except for an instant, when the monster was silhouetted against the moonlight in the central area toward which he fled. Then Louise cried, "Harry —where are you—"

Lanterns bobbed in the moonlight. The firing ceased. Wrathful Cajuns shouted, drowning the chatter of those who had survived the raid. Seagrave yelled, "Hold it, Jules! Don't shoot!"

FOR a moment, the posse forgot business; that was when Louise came into the lantern light. Seagrave hastily wrapped the remains of his coat about her. Pierre Guerin's frantic cursing subsided when he saw his daughter.

Jules Boudreaux said, "Someone told about the white *zombi* woman. Near your plantation, you

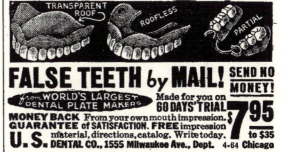

comprehend? So we think it is your fault, *hein?*"

"And you want to get me?" Seagrave cut in.

The posse was going back into the tunnel. They found Castro, face down, his head a red pulp from which bits of cracked skull protruded. Someone said, "Ah . . . this is the chief, no? And you finish him, *m'sieu* Seagrave?"

Boudreaux nodded, then went on, "Then in your cabin, we find Louise's dress. Pieces of it, you understand. We think it is bad business. Then Armand Ducoin, he saw you from his window, going to the Fort Jackson. It is simple, eh?"

"Damn simple," Seagrave said, dazed by the sudden turn. "But that big halfwit—that fake *zombi?* Where's he?"

"He jumped into the moat. With the white *zombi* woman. Just as we shoot, everybody at once. They do not come up." He shrugged. "Too many water hyacinths."

They finished what Louise had started. The wounded monster and his victim had leaped to sudden death. Seagrave shuddered. And to clear his mind of that picture, he said, "But we still don't know what it was all about, this crop of faked *zombis!*"

"Maybe these Haitian fellows will tell us," the sheriff said grinning and jerking a thumb at the black prisoners. He rubbed his hands. "Me, I will make them talk. When I hoist them down by the water moccasin in the ditch, they will say plenty."

But lantern light exposed several features of the riddle. There was a leather jerkin, and false head, which Picot wore to magnify his height, and to protect him against shots that terrified Cajuns might fire. In the same casemate, Seagrave found some sticks of low test dynamite, and a well-point. He said to Pierre Guérin, "Simple, how those graves turned inside out. Drive that point in, take it out, and shove in half a stick. Just enough of a lift to make it look as if someone came out of his coffin."

"Smart fellow, this Doctaire Castro, *hein?*" He spat a jet of tobacco. "But what for, all these *zombis?*"

In a moment, Seagrave answered that question. There was a cache of narcotics; heroin, and morphine. Judging from the labels, the stuff had been smuggled from the West Indies. When the sheriff came in to join the two, he confirmed Seagrave's suspicions. "You have reason, my fran'," he said. "These home made *zombis,* she is to scare us out of the bayou, out of the oyster fishing, out of everything. First we drive you out, then we go away too. Your plantation, she is the nize landing field for the air plane, no? And with no one living here, no one can talk too much."

Fake *zombis* to start it; two real ones to finish the terrorization of the Delta. It was simple. But so was everything else. When Seagrave heard Louise's voice, he turned and caught her in his arms. "We're going home to throw all the Pernod out the window. I've been wasting a lot of remorse."

She snuggled close, looked up and smiled. "That is not all," she murmured. "You have been waste a lot of time, *chéri. . . .*"

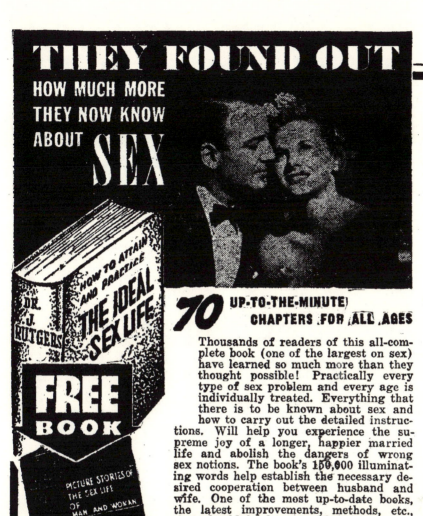
When answering advertisements please mention SPICY MYSTERY STORIES

Will o' the Wisp

[Continued from page 89]

They don't want their lovely blonde sister to be sent up. *Go get him, Helene! Drink his blood!"*

The foul, slimy swine! He was the one who'd knocked on the front door a moment ago. And I knew he must have battered Nalya's father aside, knocked him unconscious, in order to get down here to the cellar. Now he squatted like a Nero, the stairs a grandstand seat for murder . . . my murder, and perhaps Nalya's. . . .

Only it didn't work out that way. Helene, hearing Garrison's voice, turned suddenly. That was the moment I'd hoped for. I lunged at her.

But she moved a split-instant too swiftly for me. She hurled the knife; sent it arcing upward. It turned over lazily in the air, just once. Then, point-first, it buried itself in Ranse Garrison's skinny throat.

His hideous scream died as the blade sliced his larynx and severed his jugular from within. Mouth fountaining crimson, he toppled down the steps.

Helene's tattered nightgown tore as I clutched it. She slipped away from my outstretched fingers; leaned over Garrison's quivering corpse for the merest fraction of a second—just long enough to dye her mouth red-wet at his sliced throat. Then she went scurrying up the stairs, with me in frantic pursuit.

I NEVER did catch her. She made the front door just as my hand was about to close on her shoulder. Like a nude, maniac wraith she sprinted off the porch, across the welter of muddy lawn. Below, the creek was now a churning torrent of floodwater. Its current was so strong that I saw boulders and young trees being swept along—

Helene jumped far out. Her head struck horridly against an outcropping of rock. Then the stream's seething force plucked at her and carried her away. . . .

I went back into the house. Nalya was helping her father to his feet. His jaw was bruised, where Garrison had struck him down. Nalya stared at me. "Helene . . . ?"

"Gone," I said. I told her what had happened; didn't reproach her for having failed to take me into her confidence in the first place. After all, had she told me about Helene's condition when first it had evidenced itself, I would certainly have recommended some institution. And Nalya wasn't the type to put her sister away in a padded cell. I could understand why she had acted as she had. And in the final analysis, perhaps she'd been right. Helene was dead; and the man who had wrecked her sanity had reaped the recompense he deserved. What more was there than that?

So we ministered to the old man's hurts, and we left Garrison's corpse down in that flooded cellar; and then Nalya and I came very close together, and waited for the waning of the waters.

Venom Cure

[Continued from page 77]

His glance moved above the tops of the stockings, over creamy skin, smooth as velvet—and there again were the tell-tale scars.

His dark eyes brightened as he looked. For all the scientific detachment of his mind, he could not overlook the fact that her body was beautiful. He remembered how Coleman had smirked, baring her youthful bosom, and his fists clenched.

He forced a sip of brandy between her pale lips. He held a phial of aromatic ammonia beneath her nostrils. He slapped her cheeks again.

"Naida!" he called.

SHE moaned. A quiver passed through her body, stirring the white flesh of her bare thighs and the firm hills of her bosom. Her eyes flickered open—they were green-gray pools of shadow, darkened by enormous black pupils.

"Hold me close!" she begged. "I've had such awful dreams. I dreamed of Lilith—"

Lilith, mother of demons! he thought.

"Lilith was my pet," Naida went on, only half-wake. "They say snakes are horrible, but Lilith

ALL-STAR !

For nearly ten years, Dan Turner, super-sleuth with an eye for both killers and cuties in Hollywood, has appeared in every issue of

SPICY DETECTIVE

Such reader-demand must be deserved!

No SPICY-MYSTERY fan will want to miss this super-attraction—

A whole magazine full of DAN TURNER short stories and novelettes by Robert Leslie Bellem!

On all newsstands

wasn't. She went everywhere with me, and we lived well. But she died, and I couldn't find work, and I got sick, and Dr. Coleman said—"

She stopped, seeming to become aware of her surroundings. Her eyes focused on Malkin's face, and terror came into them.

"Who—who are you?"

"A friend, Naida. A doctor. Coleman brought you here."

"He told you?"

"Yes, he told me. And I have seen the marks of the fangs."

He had one arm around her, where he had started to raise her, and she snuggled sleepily against his shoulder. "It—it seems a funny way to keep alive, doesn't it? I mean, from the fangs of a snake that is supposed to be deadly? But Dr. Coleman said it was all right. He spoke of a doctor who knew a lot about snakes. Dr. Malkin. Is that you?"

"I am Dr. Malkin. I know as much about snakes as anyone in this country. I have some beauties."

"I'd love to see them. Not now, though—I'm so comfortable now. As though I were still dreaming, but not of awful things."

Her eyes were wide and innocent, and she seemed like a frail child. Gazing at her, a strange, exciting fancy came over Malkin. He had not known the love of a woman in a long time—for months now, he and Leonore had been as distant as people living at opposite poles of the earth, and he knew she would have left him before this if the thought of his wealth, which might some day be hers, had not stood in her way. But he had

missed love. He had dreamed, many times, of a woman who would understand his work and his ambitions.

And why not a girl like this? What if she were afflicted by strange desires, given over to a craving more awful than that of a morphine addict? Was not his life dedicated to the study of the forces that had made her what she was? Under the circumstances, was not her condition more a blessing than a curse?

He tightened his arm around her, and she looked up at him with a faint, mysterious smile. He bent impulsively and touched his lips to her mouth. She lay passive against him for an instant, but that first taste of a woman's lips in long months sent hot fires leaping through his veins.

Then the fires she had kindled seemed to flow back into her, and suddenly she responded with a violence that startled him. Her white arms lifted and twined about his neck. Her lips parted, returning his kisses feverishly. Her whole body arched, and the little cushions of her breast pulsed against him.

"Hold me!" she whimpered. "Hold me close!"

His glance swept down the length of her figure, and he saw her loveliness in a new light. She was no longer a patient, a subject for experiment, a human guinea pig from whom serums could be drawn after the injection of venom. For the first time since that day in India, Malkin forgot serpents, utterly and completely. He forgot his work, his painstaking experiments. He forgot Leonore,

"So That's Where He Gets His Ideas!"

THE PLAYBOY'S HANDBOOK
or
A Guide To Faster Living
By George (The Real) McCoy

Here are gathered in one pleasure-laden volume, all the indispensable fittings for every gay buckaroo. An open guide to fun and frolic—to a rakish reputation—and to a maiden's heart. The sailor has his girl in every port, the salesman has his farmer's daughter in every hamlet—but YOU can have THE PLAYBOY'S HANDBOOK with you all the time!

NOT FOR GOODY-GOODS
But Good For Others

Contains such rare and exhilarating gems as:—Advice to a Young Man on the Choice of a Maiden—How to Have Fun with Your Clothes On—The Technique of Manly Persuasion—Wit, Wisdom and Wickedness—Kissing Is a National Pastime, etc.—plus a tremendous collection of Witty, Ribald and Rowdy—Jingles, Songs, Ballads, Tales, Anecdotes, Stories, Recitations, Limericks, Jokes, Situations,

KNICKERBOCKER PUB. CO.
Dept. P16E, 98 Liberty St., New York, N. Y.

Illustrations, Drawings, and Art—to tickle the fancy of every man with hair on his chest!

Do not deny yourself the enjoyment of these keyhole frivolities and instructions. Send for your copy now. The price is only $1.00—the enjoyment is a thousandfold. Sent in plain wrapper. Money back guarantee. Mail coupon NOW.

and all the world except Naida.

"Sweet!" he whispered. "You'll stay with me always, won't you?"

She said: "Always."

Her body was like fluid flame against him. Her kisses were burning, scalding shivers of delirium.

SAPRANI was jealous. Saprani writhed and hissed behind the glass of her cage, and all the other serpents of the room hissed their hatred with her. Saprani poised her dark head and drove it toward the figures on the couch, and her fangs thudded loudly against the glass. Two milky streams of venom trickled downward. . . .

"She hates me," the girl said rapturously, "but I love her! She's like Lilith—only she's larger, more beautiful. And I know how to make her love me, if you have an Indian flute."

Reeves Malkin arose, still faint with the ecstasy that had been upon him, and took a long reed from a shelf. He handed it to the girl, and she went immediately to the cage and knelt before it. Saprani struck again at the glass, and then the girl lifted the reed to her lips and ran her fingers lightly over the stops.

The thin, lilting strains of the *sappa wallah's* tune lifted in the little chamber, and gradually all the sounds of hissing ceased, and even the squat lizards seemed entranced.

A slow ripple passed through the twelve-foot body of the Queen Cobra. She drew herself into graceful jet-black coils, out of which lifted the flat diamond head with the golden spangles like pendant earrings. Higher the head lift-

ed, till it towered almost to the top of the cage, higher than the head of the girl. The great hood spread and quivered, its veins of crimson swelling and receding. The incandescent eyes held a light of unholy joy.

The Daughter of Hell, whose kiss is the crowning finality, began to dance!

"Open the cage," breathed Naida, without interrupting the slow rhythm of the melody.

Slowly Malkin turned the crank that raised the heavy pane of glass. It lifted until its lower edge met the top of the cage, where it rested upon a tiny latch. Now there was nothing between the kneeling, half-naked girl and the deadliest of all the creatures that walk or fly or creep—nothing except the magic of music.

Saprani swayed like an undulating column of smoke, twisting and weaving. Her pink mouth was open wide, baring the tiny horn-like fangs, between which the tongue was a darting arrow, vibrant and blurred. Her ebony scales reflected the light in silver gleams.

"Marvelous!" exclaimed Malkin, enthralled by the satanic ritual. "You're better at that than I am, Naida—and as good as any I've seen in India."

He leaned forward, and inadvertently touched the tiny catch that held open the glass panel. The catch slipped into its slot and the heavy door plunged downward four feet. On its way, it struck the arched neck of the serpent a glancing blow, causing the creature to withdraw itself with the swiftness of lightning into the cage. Then the sheet struck the concrete floor with a force that shattered it and a sound that echoed throughout the house.

Naida screamed briefly. She flung up her hands to shield her face from flying splinters of glass, and the reed dropped from her fingers. Within the open cage Saprani poised for a split second, then launched a blow no eye could follow.

MALKIN saw Naida flung back upon her shoulders as though a fist had felled her. He saw the writhing thickness of the cobra lying across her, and the open mouth of the cobra fastened to her snowy flesh. He heard her scream again, and for a moment horror held him motionless.

Then, with a surge of relief, he remembered that the venom could not harm her—that it would stimulate and reinvigorate her temporarily, whatever might be its ultimate effects. It had been so with the brown girl at the ruined temple in India. It had been so in another case he knew.

Gently he stooped above Saprani. He grasped her just back of the head, and her shimmering coils went limp. He lifted her, panting a little with her weight, and deposited her in another empty cage against the wall.

He touched Naida. He said: "Don't be frightened, dearest. It's over. The venom can't hurt you."

He frowned. A taut shudder—a convulsion—went through her limbs. He looked at her eyes, and they had rolled upward in their sockets until their pupils were invisible. Her jaw was sagging. He

NOTE: This Book will not be sold to anyone below 21 years.

Size of book is 9½ x 6½ inches; beautifully printed in clear type; 151 pages with Illustrations; HARD COVER; cloth binding.

FORMER PRICE $3.00

NOW ONLY 98¢

"SEX SECRETS of LOVE and MARRIAGE"

Daringly Revealed

Edited by Dr. Edward Podolsky

This is an enlightened age. Are you one of those, still *afraid to know the truth* about the many intimate questions of man or woman? Or are you one of those who thinks—"I know it all"—and is actually unaware of many important facts and pleasures. Do you know how to live a complete, vigorous and delightful sex life? Do you know your part in the game of love? Every happy marriage is based, to a great extent, on a happy sex life. But how can you lead a satisfactory love life, if you do not know—or are not sure, of the many, many facts and ways of love, of marriage, of sex—of the 1000 ways of a man with a woman! Are you getting ALL that you expected, that you dreamed of—from your love, from your marriage, from your life? Or are *doubts* and *difficulties* in the art of love troubling you, holding you back, spoiling everything.

Offers a Liberal Education in Sexual Science

At last, the whole truth about sex! The time has come to bring this intimate and necessary knowledge into the light of day—into the hands of every adult man and woman who wants to lead a satisfactory, healthy, full love life. Written in simple and frank language—SECRETS OF LOVE AND MARRIAGE explains: How to attract the opposite sex—how to win love—how to conduct yourself during your honeymoon. The book teaches the proper sexual conduct in marriage and the technique of the sex act. The book explains: the problems of the wife and how to solve them—and the problems of the husbands and how to overcome them. Sometimes they are actual physical disabilities, such as impotence, sterility, etc. The book advises you on correcting these difficulties. It also devotes a chapter to "BIRTH CONTROL," with reasons for and against—and the method of accomplishing. It features a table of "safe periods." It explains conception, pregnancy. In short, it is a complete teacher and guide on practically every phase of Love—Marriage—and SEX!

"Secrets of Love and Marriage" is an endless source of intimate, intriguing information, from the first awakening of youthful love to the full flowering of grand passion . . . answering many questions you hesitate to ask even your closest friends. You must know the real facts and ways or be cheated out of life's most precious pleasures!

Let Us Send You This Book on Trial!

Send no money now. Just mail the coupon. When book arrives, deposit with postman only 98c plus shipping charges, under our MONEY BACK GUARANTEE. You risk nothing. Mail coupon now.

felt for her pulse, and swore a mighty oath.

Saprani's kiss of death was—fatal.

He stumbled into the laboratory, only half aware of his purpose. He lifted down a small jar of yellowish, slimy fluid. He ighted the blue flame of a bunsen burner, poured some of the fluid into a test tube and heated it over the flame. He mixed in a white powder and stirred it, and added water until the mixture was thin and pale.

It was a forlorn gesture, made almost automatically. Even if he had prepared this serum in advance against the possible fatal consequences of the venom he would hardly have thought it worth using. He had made it of the blood of a dog injected little by little with infinitesimal quantities of venom, and of his own blood and some of the blood of Saprani, who was impervious to her own poison. He had added strychnine and other heart stimulants.

The stuff had been an utter failure in a dozen tests.

Nevertheless, Malkin sterilized and filled a large hypodermic needle with the stuff. He rushed back into the smaller room, spilled alcohol over Naida's wrist and jabbed the point of the needle into one of the large veins of the forearm. There was no spurt of blood—only a slow trickle, unspeeded by any perceptible pulse.

When he had shot the hot serum into her vein, he lifted her to the couch. He rubbed her arms and her side near her heart, moved her limbs and tried by every means he knew to induce heart action. He worked for frantic minutes, while sweat beaded his forehead and dampened all his body.

Then he gave it up. He stood for other minutes, dully contemplating the still form, remembering how it had pulsed with life and ardor so recently. Greater even than his sense of loss was his feeling of infinite pity for this girl who, in some manner, had been made the innocent victim of ghastly trickery.

Then came the thought of the man who must have conceived the fatal trick, and the understanding of that man's motive. Anger, cold and icy, froze all other emotions. That man was Roy Coleman, Leonore's secret lover—and that man was here, within reach.

Malkin lifted the glass front of the cage in which he had placed the cobra. He reached for her with both arms, grasping her scaly coils. She hissed and struck, not angrily, burying her fangs in his chest, and he felt the sting of her venom mingle with his blood.

He laughed bitterly. "Save it, Saprani," he muttered. "I have other work for you."

ROY COLEMAN and Leonore Malkin laughed softly together. They sat, half reclining, upon a chaise longue, and the young man's arms embraced her. The light wrapper she wore had been allowed to come unfastened, and a whole side of her softly rounded white body was bare—curving waist, gleaming hip, and tapering thigh. Coleman's eyes sparkled, missing no detail, and he kept moistening his too-red lips with his tongue.

"That crash we heard a few min-

When answering advertisements please mention SPICY MYSTERY STORIES

utes ago means that something is happening," Coleman said. "I don't think we'll have to wait long. Darling, the firelight on your skin is beautiful!"

"Never mind my skin," she replied. "Not now, I mean. I won't be able to think of anything else till it's over. If Reeves should suspect anything, he might get violent."

"How can he suspect, Leonore? The girl is so full of dope she can't be coherent. Besides the morphine, I gave her that extra shot of *cannabis Indica* when I brought her in here. The effect of that drug— it's really just plain hasheesh— is to intensify any emotion or idea that comes into the subject's head, or is put into it. For instance, if Reeves should try to make love to her, she would grow wild with ardor in a second." He chuckled. "Imagine Reeves making love to a girl!"

"He might," Leonore said. "He used to. To me, I mean—before we began to quarrel so much."

"He's too daffy about snakes now," Coleman declared. "And that's another thing in our favor. The girl actually knows snakes— used to own 'em and make 'em sit up. You know—Hindu stuff. So when he talks about snakes, and she remembers that I always gave her the dope she craved through a rattle-snake's fangs, the rest will be simple. She really thinks it was a venom extract I gave her."

"How could she be so stupid, Roy?"

He shrugged. "It was natural enough. She came to me with those neuralgic pains, and told me something about herself. Right away I

saw how I could use her. Instead of the regular treatment for neuralgia, I gave her morphine, which dulled the pain. I used the jaw of a snake for the injections, and kept increasing the doses till she simply had to have the stuff or go nuts. I scarred up her body so my story would be more plausible. Then, when I thought the time was ripe, I drove her here and told Reeves I'd discovered exactly the kind of case he'd written about finding in India." He chuckled again. "I'm surprised he fell for those Hindu superstitions!"

"But what if the girl doesn't die?"

"She's got to, honey. Nothing can stop cobra venom. If you're bitten on the wrist, the only thing to do is chop off your arm right away. It only takes seconds for the stuff to go through your system. It changes the structure of the blood—curdles it, actually. And if Reeves doesn't try cobra venom on her, with the build-up I've given the case, I've been so dumb I don't deserve to get you and the—"

"Go ahead. Say it. The money, you mean. Well, he has over half a million dollars in bonds and cash and property. If only we can get our hands on it, I won't mind you being a little bit greedy."

"We'll get our hands on it, all right. If they don't send him to prison or the chair for murder, they'll find him dangerously insane. You'll have charge of the estate, naturally, and can do what you want with it. Or, if the worst comes to the worst, you can claim your lawful third of it—the 'widow's portion.' In cases of insanity, it's proper to make such a claim, or a larger one."

She said: "We could live high, wide and handsome even on that much, dear. And do I want to live that way, after being cooped up here!"

"Hush!" he said. "I thought I heard—"

REEVES MALKIN came into the room. They faced him simultaneously, and Coleman sprang to his feet and stood rigid with terror. Leonore screamed briefly and cowered where she was. The eyes of both were horror-stricken.

Malkin's face was more cadaverous than ever in the dim firelight that sent shifting shadows across the room. His eyes blazed, but even they were like the eyes of a devil, not a man. His figure was skeletal, and the hideousness of his appearance was heightened by the sleek coils of the great serpent draped about his shoulders and waist, and the fatal jaws of the serpent, thrust against the blood-soaked front of his shirt.

Malkin said hollowly: "She's dead. Saprani bit her, and she died."

Coleman's voice had become a quavering falsetto. "But — my God, man!—are you committing suicide because of that? Are you letting the snake bite you to death because it killed her?" His tones were laden with dread, but there was a note of hope in them, too, and a light of eagerness showed in Leonore's face.

Malkin shook his head slowly. "No. You see, knowledge of *mar-*

Boxing the Compass
with
Thrilling Adventure

Red-blooded men and warm-hearted women will thrill to the exploits of fiction's greatest array of adventurers. From the steppes of Russia to the warm, rapturous islands of the South Seas; from the Bering Sea to Borneo, life is filled with romance and intrigue.

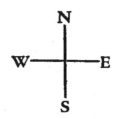

If you want Real Life in its most exciting moments don't fail to buy a copy of

Spicy-Adventure Stories

ON SALE EVERYWHERE

ashakh, the venom-fever, is based on fact. Saprani's venom will not harm me." He tore at his shirt, shredding it. "These blue marks on my shoulder are where the first cobra bit me in India, just before I came down with that sickness. These others on my chest—the old ones and the fresher ones—are where Saprani administered to me as often as I felt the need of more venom to counterbalance the anti-venom that had formed in my blood."

Coleman's face was ashen. "But —then—"

"I heard what you were saying before I came in," Malkin interrupted. "It wasn't I who murdered Naida Marsh—it was the pair of you. But I know what you would say to the authorities, and how easily you could slip out of it, and so I am sentencing you, myself. As she died, you shall die."

"No!" Leonore shrieked. "For God's sake, Reeves—no!"

"You will have a chance for life." Malkin plucked Saprani's fangs from his chest, stroked the back of her head and lifted her limp coils from his body. He placed the serpent on a table eight feet from the chaise longue. The instant he took his hands from her, she coiled again and reared her head and hissed.

"She smells your fear," Malkin said. "Yet she will not strike you as long as you remain perfectly still. But the instant you move, she will hit you before you know it. Death will come within seconds, but the agony will be terrible while it is coming."

"But—" Coleman began.

"No talk," Malkin warned.

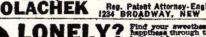

When answering advertisements please mention SPICY MYSTERY STORIES

"Talk will excite her, too." He moved slowly toward the door. "I'll come back in two hours, and if you are still alive, I'll take Saprani away and let you go. If you're dead, I'll simply say one of my specimens got out of its cage and went roaming through the house, and you were unlucky enough to meet it."

He left the room without a backward glance at the frozen figures of the semi-nude woman and the craven physician, who had thought to loose death on others, and now were face to face with death for as long as their wavering nerves could stand the awful strain. He knew with cold certainty it would not be very long. . . .

SOMBER thoughts filled Malkin's mind as he descended the cellar steps into the laboratory. He was not worried about his own safety — the presence of three corpses in his house could easily be explained by the story of a gruesome accident which loosed the deadly cobra. But he dreaded going ahead alone, with the memory of Naida haunting him, and at least some of the guilt for her death burdening his soul.

He would go on, of course. Much as the world might laugh, he was on the verge of a great and important discovery. He had thought more than once he was on the point of succeeding with his serums— but something had gone wrong each time. Still, the next time might well be different.

He had no fear of the serpent gods of India. The venom might kill him in time, if he did not reach the end of his experiments soon—but, now that this had happened, it would not matter. Still, he had found in his tests of himself that he could regulate the amount of venom he required to keep in health—could reduce or increase it at will, without bad effects. Once his goal was reached, he could cure himself of *mar ashakh,* if there were any reason for wanting to be cured.

Now, if Naida had not died. . . . She had lived for weeks or months on a morphine diet, but that was not a bad thing to cure—not as bad as though she had been a conscious addict for years. He could have cured her, he was certain. And she had been sweet, where Leonore had been only proud and selfish. He knew instinctively that they would have been happy together.

If Saprani had not killed her. . . .

He pushed open the door to the little chamber, and the hisses of a hundred reptiles greeted him. He looked toward the couch and halted, transfixed by astonishment.

Naida was sitting on the edge of the couch, her face in her hands. At the sound of the door opening she turned a wan face toward him.

"I feel sick," she complained. "Dizzy. I dreamed that I had died and come to life again. Dr. Malkin —did the cobra bite me, or did I dream it? There seems to be a fresh wound in my chest—"

A loud, joyful cry burst from him. "My serum! It's a success!" His mind went back over the things he had added to it a few minutes ago—the strychnine and other heart stimulants. By God, he had it, at last!

He knelt beside her, clasping

her in his arms. "We've done it!" he exulted. "You and I! We've saved lives without number, Naida—and now we have only to save our own. Together we can do it."

She was tired. Her head drooped against his shoulder. She murmured wearily: "Together."

Her body was warm against him, and he thought her the most beautiful thing he had ever seen. He tightened his arms and held her tenderly closer.

The hissing of the snakes and lizards ceased. Only the sounds of the rising storm came into the room.

The uproar drowned lesser sounds in another part of the house —noises of furniture being overturned, voices lifting in frenzied shrieks, sobs and moans of anguish, feeble prayers and curses dying away into silence, the sibilant hiss of the triumphant Saprani. . . .

Classified Section

Have you bought your Bonds today?

Do your share to win your War!

759681

Made in the USA